Father CHRISTMAS And Me

Father CHRISTMAS And Me

MATT HAIG

with illustrations by CHRIS MOULD

CANONGATE

Published in Great Britain in 2017 by Canongate Books Ltd,
14 High Street, Edinburgh EH1 1TE

canongate.co.uk

1

British Library Cataloguing-in-Publication Data
A catalogue record for this book is available on
request from the British Library

ISBN 978 1 78689 068 9

Typeset in 13.25/15pt Bembo by
Palimpsest Book Production Ltd, Falkirk, Stirlingshire

Printed and bound in Great Britain by Clays Ltd, St Ives plc.

For Pearl, Lucas and Andrea

Somewhere Else

Y2ou might think you know about Father Christmas. And I'm sure you do know *some* things. You probably know about the Toy Workshop and the reindeer. You know what happens every Christmas Eve. Of course you do.

But the thing you probably don't know about is me.

I will start by telling you the things that are easy to believe.

My name is Amelia Wishart and I have a black cat called Captain Soot. I was born in London, and I lived there until I was eleven years old. And then I lived *somewhere else*.

It is the *somewhere else* that you might find a bit unlikely.

I suppose I could tell you that I moved to Finland, and you would have no problem believing that, because Finland is on a map. And it is, technically, true. I did move to Finland, in the far far *far* North,

beyond the bit of Finland known as Lapland. The *somewhere else* I lived was simply called the Far North and the town was Elfhelm. Now, Elfhelm isn't on any maps. Not human ones, anyway. And the reason for this is that *most people can't see it.* It's *invisible* to them. You see, Elfhelm is a magical place, and to see magical places you have to believe in magic. And the type of humans who draw all the maps are the people least likely to believe in magic.

But Elfhelm is an ordinary town in lots of ways. A small town. An oversized village, really. And there are normal things there, like shops and houses and a town hall. There are streets and trees and even a bank.

But the people who live there are *very* different to me. And *very* different to you too.

They aren't even people. Not *human* people anyway.

They are special. They are magic.

They are, well . . .

They are elves. But the thing is, if you are surrounded by elves, it isn't the elves that are the weird, unusual creatures.

No.

It's you.

7 *Reindeer Road*

ather Christmas lived at 7 Reindeer Road, right next to Reindeer Field, on the edge of Elfhelm.

His house, like many of the houses in Elfhelm, was made of reinforced gingerbread, and – unlike almost all other houses in Elfhelm – it had a front door so large you didn't have to bend forwards to walk through it.

It was full of fun things. There was a slide down from the first floor to the ground floor. The doorbell played a version of 'Jingle Bells'. There were toys everywhere. The kitchen had shelves full of the tastiest sweet things in jars – chocolate, gingerbread, cloudberry jam. There was a reindeer clock in the living room, which was like a cuckoo clock but instead of a cuckoo popping out it was a reindeer. Oh, and it didn't tell ordinary human time with boring things like 'six o'clock' and 'twenty past nine'. It told elf time, and elf hours were called things like Very Early Indeed and Way Past Bedtime.

Father Christmas had been living on his own but he quickly got Slumber, the elf bedmaker, to build two extra beds and 'the world's comfiest cat basket' for Captain Soot.

'Though tonight,' he said that first day, 'I'll sleep downstairs on the trampoline.' Father Christmas insisted that it was a very comfy trampoline.

The reason Father Christmas needed two extra beds was because of Mary Ethel Winters and myself.

Mary was the woman Father Christmas was in love with. He blushed every time he looked at her. And she loved him too.

Mary was the kindest and loveliest woman
I had ever met. Her cheeks were as rosy as
apples and her smile could warm a room. I
had first known her when I was in London,
when the very worst thing of all happened.
My mother caught a horrible illness from
cleaning chimneys. I did all I could to look
after her, but in the end the illness was too
powerful. I couldn't stop her dying. My father
had left us when I was very little, so after that
I was sent to Mr Jeremiah Creeper's workhouse.
I was utterly miserable, but Mary – who worked

in the kitchens there – was always nice to me. She would secretly add a spoonful of honey to the watery gruel we had to eat. I'll never forget that.

She'd had a tough life. Before she had gone to the workhouse she had been homeless and slept on a bench next to Tower Bridge, surrounded by pigeons.

Anyway, when Captain Soot and I eventually escaped the workhouse, thanks to Father Christmas, Mary came with us. And, like me, she was very pleased to be here.

We arrived in Elfhelm on Christmas Day, when every human child in the world was opening their presents, and we ate the biggest Christmas dinner I had ever seen and listened to the most brilliant and happy music played by an elf band called the Sleigh Belles. We laughed and sang and spickle danced. Spickle dancing is a very complicated type of elf dancing which involves a lot of energetic leg work, a lot of twisting, and some floating magically in the air.

'I think you are going to like it here,' Father Christmas told me later, as we went ice skating on a frozen lake.

'Yes, I think I will,' I said.

And I did. I did like it there. Well for a while.
Before I managed to smash my own happiness
into a million pieces.

Hope Toffee

To get anywhere in Elfhelm you had to walk along a big street called the Main Path. Elves weren't always very original with their names. For instance, there was another street with seven curves that they called the Street of Seven Curves.

Anyway, as we walked along the Main Path the whole street was bustling with elves. There were clog shops, tunic shops, belt shops. There was something called the School of Sleighcraft on the Main Path too. All kinds of sleighs were there, though none looked as impressive as the one I had ridden on my journey to Elfhelm – the one Father Christmas kept parked in Reindeer Field.

Father Christmas waved at a tall (by elf standards), skinny elf who was polishing a small white sleigh. The sleigh gleamed and looked quite beautiful.

'Hello, Kip! Is that the new sleigh I've been hearing about?'

The elf smiled. It was a small smile. The kind of smile that was surprised to be there. 'Yes, Father Christmas. The Blizzard 360.'

'She looks a beauty. Single-reindeer?'

'Yes, single-reindeer.'

And then Father Christmas started on a long and technical conversation about speedometers and harnesses and altitude gauges and compasses.

He finished their discussion with a question: 'So you'll be letting the children ride in it when the school term starts?'

Kip looked worried suddenly. 'No,' he said.

'This isn't a child's sleigh. Look at the size of it. This is for bigger elves – grown-ups only.'

Then Mary joined in. 'Well,' she said, putting her arm around me, 'the school is getting a new child this year. A child who is bigger than an elf child. A child who is actually taller than an elf grown-up.'

'This is Amelia,' added Father Christmas, 'and believe me, she is a natural sleigh rider.'

Kip stared at me and turned as pale as snow. 'Oh. I see. Um. Err. Right. Well.'

And that was it. He went back to polishing his sleigh and we carried on walking along the street.

'Poor Kip,' said Father Christmas softly. 'He had a terrible childhood.'

Every other elf we saw was very friendly and talkative. Mother Breer the beltmaker fitted Father Christmas with a new belt. ('Oh, Father Christmas, your belly has *grown*. We're going to have to make an extra hole.')

Then we went to the sweet shop and met Bonbon the sweetmaker, who let us taste some of the new things she had been working on. We tried the Purple Cloudberry Fudge and a strong-tasting aniseed-y sweet called Blitzen's Revenge (named after Father Christmas's favourite reindeer) and then the Baby Soother.

'Why is it called the Baby Soother?' I asked. And then she pointed to her baby – 'little Suki' – who had a cute face and pointed ears, and was sitting happily in a bouncy chair, sucking on a sweet.

'It always works on her,' said Bonbon.

The most incredible sweet of all, though, was the one called Hope Toffee.

'Ooh, toffee,' I said, clapping my hands. 'I love toffee. What does this one taste of?'

Bonbon looked at me as if I had said something very stupid. 'It is *Hope* Toffee. It tastes of whatever you hope it tastes like.'

So when I put it in my mouth I hoped very hard that it would taste like chocolate, and it did taste like chocolate, and then I hoped it would taste like apple pie, and the sweet heated up in my mouth and became exactly like apple pie, and then I thought of the roasted chestnuts I used to eat every Christmas, before Mother had become poorly, and there they were, tender and warm and crumbling like a memory in my mouth. And this last taste, although delicious, also made me feel sad that I didn't have a mother any more, so I swallowed it and didn't ask for another one. I had some Giggle Candy instead, which tickled my tongue and made me laugh.

The shop doorbell tinkled and in walked a smartly dressed couple, both wearing red tunics. One of them had glasses and a bald head, and the other was as round as a globe.

'Ah, hello, Pi,' said Father Christmas to the one with glasses.

He then turned to me. 'Pi is your new mathematics teacher.'

'Hello,' Pi said, chewing on some liquorice. 'You're a human. I've heard about human mathematics. It sounds most ridiculous.'

I was confused. 'I thought mathematics was the same everywhere.'

Pi laughed. 'Quite the opposite! Quite the opposite!'

And then I was introduced to the other elf, who was called Columbus. 'I'm a teacher too. I teach geography.'

'Is elf geography like human geography?' asked Mary.

But Father Christmas answered on Columbus's behalf. 'No. For one thing, in human geography, Elfhelm doesn't even exist.'

And then we ate some more sweets and bought some to take home and said goodbye to Bonbon and Pi and Columbus and headed out into the street. We walked past a newspaper stand selling the *Daily Snow*.

'Oh dear,' said Father Christmas. 'There's no queue . . . No one wants to buy the *Daily Snow* any more.'

I knew a bit about the *Daily Snow*. It was the main elf newspaper. It had always been run by an elf called Father Vodol. Father Vodol was a Very Bad Elf. He'd always hated Father Christmas and, when Father Christmas had first arrived in Elfhelm as a boy, had locked him up in prison. You see, Father Vodol used to be the Leader of the Elf Council and had ruled Elfhelm and made everyone fear outsiders, such as humans. But then, when Father Christmas had become Leader, Father Vodol kept running the *Daily Snow* for years – until last Christmas, when it became clear he'd helped the trolls attack Elfhelm. His punishment hadn't been prison (elves don't go to prison any more), it had been to lose the *Daily Snow* and to go and live in a small house on the quietest street in Elfhelm, which was called Very Quiet Street. It was seen as a punishment to have to live on Very Quiet Street because elves *hated* the quiet.

The only trouble with the *Daily Snow* was that since Noosh, the former Reindeer Correspondent, had taken over, two things had happened. First, the newspaper had got a lot better. Second, it had also stopped selling. It seemed that elves preferred it when Father Vodol made up stories and lied about everything.

I am telling you all this now, because it is important for what happens later. But at the time – stepping out of that sweet shop – I had a different worry in my mind.

'I have never been to a school before. They didn't teach you anything in the workhouse. All you did was work. And, besides, elf school sounds very strange. How will I fit in?'

'Oh, but you see,' said Father Christmas,

'you underestimate yourself. You were good at riding a sleigh right from the start, weren't you?'

'But what if—'

'Listen,' said Father Christmas. 'You don't have to worry. This is *Elfhelm*. This is the place where anything can happen. It's like that sweet you just ate. Whatever you hope to feel, you *will* feel.'

'Is life really that simple, Nikolas?' asked Mary, who called Father Christmas by his first name.

'It can be,' said Father Christmas.

And it was easy to feel as positive as him, right then, as we walked down the Main Path. Everything looked happy and bright.

Just then I noticed Father Christmas and Mary holding hands, and I thought it looked a very lovely thing. Maybe the loveliest thing I had ever seen. And I was so overwhelmed with the loveliness of it that I found myself saying what was in my mind, and what was in my mind was this: 'You should get married.'

Both of them turned around to look at me on that happy, bustling, snow-lined street and looked shocked.

'Sorry,' I said, 'I shouldn't have said that.'

They looked at each other and burst out laughing.

And Mary said, 'What a good idea, Amelia!'

And Father Christmas said, 'The very best idea!'

And that is how Mary Ethel Winters came to marry Father Christmas.

Mother Christmas

The wedding took place on the last day of the winter holidays. The day before I was due to start at Elfhelm School. It had been nice to have the wedding to look forward to, as it had taken my mind off starting school.

Most of Elfhelm came to the Village Hall that day. Some pixies from the Wooded Hills even came. The Truth Pixie was there along with the Lie Pixie. The Lie Pixie said that he really liked my ears, which was a bit worrying. Father Christmas's reindeer were all there too. He had made Blitzen promise that he wouldn't go to the toilet on the floor during the service, and Blitzen stuck to that promise. There was also a Tomtegubb there. I had heard of pixies and elves, even when I had lived in London, but I had never heard of Tomtegubbs. There weren't many of them apparently, and they were only found to the east of Elfhelm. Tomtegubbs didn't have names and they were never male or female. They were always just

Tomtegubbs and they came in different colours. This one glowed a kind of yellow and was a short chubby thing, and it smiled and hummed to itself the whole time. And Captain Soot came along too, nibbling dropped cake crumbs from the floor.

Oh, and there was also an earthquake. Or what felt like an earthquake. But it turned out to be just a troll walking all the way from Troll Valley to the wedding. She was such a large troll she couldn't actually fit in the hall and had to sit on the snowy ground outside, but she peered inside the window. This was Urgula, the Supreme Troll Leader, who was larger even than all the untertrolls and übertrolls she was in charge of. I didn't see the whole of her, but I saw her head with her hair as wild as a tree blowing in the wind.

Father Christmas opened the window at one point to talk to her. 'Hello, Urgula, lovely to see you here.'

Urgula smiled and showed her three teeth, each one the size of a rotten door. 'I be here to wish you and your love the biggest happiness from all we trolls.'

'That is very kind,' said Mary, standing by Father Christmas's side.

The Sleigh Belles played a song they had written for the occasion called 'You Look Beautiful To Me My Sweetheart (Even Though You Are A Human)'.

Father Topo, Father Christmas's best friend, led the service. Elfhelm weddings, I soon realised, were slightly different to human ones.

'Look into each other's eyes,' said Father Topo, 'and try not to laugh.'

They both managed that very well until Father Topo started telling some terrible jokes.

'What's the best Christmas present?'

'I don't know,' said Mary.

'A broken drum! You just can't beat it . . . Get it?'

'Yes,' said Father Christmas, 'I told you that one!'

But Father Topo had more.

'What says "oh oh oh"? You walking backwards . . . Get it? Because you normally say "ho ho ho". Okay. Why couldn't the skeleton go to the party? Because he had no body to go with. No body! See? What's a human child's favourite king? A stocking . . .' And these terrible jokes went on for quite some time. Until eventually both Father Christmas and Mary were laughing – not because the jokes were so funny, but because they were so bad. And it was at that moment – that exact moment of laughing-at-the-same-time-ness – that Father Topo said, 'I now pronounce you MARRIED!' Because that is how people get married in Elfhelm. By laughing together at the same time in the middle of a wedding service.

Mary became Mother Christmas automatically because Father Christmas was the Leader of the Elf Council. And Mary became a member of the Elf Council, too. That was why some people were called Mother Something or Father Something. They were members of the Elf Council, which meant they could attend

meetings and help to decide things to do with Elfhelm and elf life. Anyone, in theory, could be a member of the Elf Council. It just so happened that a lot of elves never wanted to be, because meetings were known to be boring and to give them rashes. And very itchy rashes at that.

After the talking part of the wedding, there was the food part (a *lot* of food), and more music, and even more spickle dancing.

Towards the end of the party a grumpy-looking elf with a black beard appeared and wandered through the crowd, scowling at Father Christmas and Mary – or Mother Christmas – and at anyone who seemed to be happy. Which was absolutely everybody in the room apart from the Truth Pixie, who seemed to want Father Christmas to stay on his own (I knew this because I overheard her saying 'I wish Father Christmas would stay on his own'), so this was a bit of a difficult day for her.

'Are you having a good time?' I asked the Truth Pixie innocently.

'I am having the worst day of my life,' she responded, before stuffing her face with wedding cake.

The scowling elf was Father Vodol. When Father Christmas raised his glass to make a toast at the end, I watched Father Vodol staring intently at Father Christmas's cup of cloudberry juice.

'Dear elves, pixies, humans, reindeer, troll – oh, and you Tomtegubb – thank you all for coming. Today has been very special for me. Like a million Christmas Days all at once. Because I have married the kindest, warmest and funniest person I have ever known – that's you, Mother Christmas – and I am surrounded by all of you. I would also like to mention someone else in the room.' That was when he pointed at me. 'That person there. Amelia Wishart. The girl who saved Christmas. She has taught me a lot. Mostly she has taught me the power of hope. As you know, hope is a kind of magic. And it is now my great hope and belief that Elfhelm will continue to welcome her – and my dear Mary – into our village, as you have done already. Like me, they may look a little different, but I assure you they will add much to life here in Elfhelm.'

'Here, here,' said Noosh, now standing next to her great-great-great-great-great-grandfather, Father Topo, and holding her son, Little Mim, in her arms.

'Absolutely,' said Father Topo. 'Elfhelm is more fun if it welcomes everyone. A village full of only elves is as boring as a stocking filled with the same presents.'

'Well, I am very happy to be here,' said Mary. 'And I know Amelia is too. Aren't you, Amelia?'

The whole hall turned to look at me.

'Oh yes,' I said. 'I am very happy. It certainly beats a workhouse, I can tell you.'

The elves smiled at me but there was a look of confusion or perhaps it was amusement in their faces. I guess it was because I was *different*. I was different even to Mary and Father

Christmas. There was no drimwickery inside me. Drimwickery is elf magic. A magic that had been used to save the life of Father Christmas when he was a boy, and which he in turn had used to save Mary's life last Christmas. I couldn't do the things that elves and Father Christmas and Mary – once she'd completed her drimwick classes – could do. But I didn't care. Not yet, anyway. I quite liked being different. All my life, in London, I had been invisible. Just another poor scruffy sooty-faced child. It was nice to be looked at. It made me feel a bit special, and I had never felt special before.

And Father Christmas helped me out by saying, 'So let's raise our glasses to happiness and friendship! It doesn't matter who anyone is, or where they have come from, they are here in Elfhelm and we will welcome them.'

Father Vodol, I realised, was still staring at the goblet in Father Christmas's hand. And, as he stared at it, I saw that goblet begin to tremble and shake, and Father Christmas seemed shocked as he tried to keep hold of it. But it was no good. The goblet whooshed across the room and landed with a loud clank near my feet. I looked down to see pink-orange cloudberry juice spill out.

No one realised it had been Father Vodol, because no one had been watching how intensely he had been staring at Father Christmas.

'What happened there?' Mary asked.

'I have no idea,' said Father Christmas.

'It was him,' I said and pointed to the black-bearded culprit.

The whole hall suddenly went very quiet. Everyone looked a bit worried, including Father Christmas. And then, I started to feel a little worried too. 'It was Father V—'

But I couldn't finish my sentence as my

mouth was jammed shut. My lips were forced together yet no one was touching them.

It was then I realised: *he* was doing it.

'I have no idea what the human girl is talking about,' said Father Vodol, with a smile. 'She is clearly mistaken.'

I tried to speak but I couldn't. I looked at Father Christmas's and Mary's troubled faces. I didn't want to ruin their special day, so I just shrugged and gave a tight-lipped smile.

Father Christmas looked at his now empty hand and at the puddle on the floor beside my feet. He pushed out his bottom lip. 'Well let's not cry about spilled juice. We are here to celebrate.' He clapped his hands. 'Sleigh Belles, play us another tune.'

The music began again, and elves filled the dancefloor, and there was some rather competitive spickle dancing going on. And I danced too, in a rather unmagical human way, until Father Vodol came and stood right in front of me.

I was a little bit frightened but was determined not to show it. So I said, 'Do you like dancing?'

And he said, 'No, I don't. You see, the trouble is you have to watch your step. And if you put a foot wrong there can be consequences.'

I laughed. 'I don't think dancing has to be so serious.'

But then I realised he wasn't talking about dancing, because he said, 'I'm not talking about dancing.'

'Oh.'

'I'm talking about you.'

'Why do I have to watch my step?'

'Because your feet are too big.'

'What? This is precisely how my feet are meant to be. I'm a human.'

'*Exactly.*' His eyes widened. He looked quite mad. 'You are a human. You do not belong here.'

'Father Christmas is a human. Mary is a human. Don't they belong here? All the other elves seem to think so.'

He leaned in closer, so he could speak quietly but still be heard above the music. 'Oh, you don't understand the mind of elves. You see, they are very changeable. You take one wrong step and they'll turn against you. You'll see. I'll make sure of it.'

'I'm not scared of you.'

'Yet,' he said. 'You're not scared of me *yet*. Just watch those big feet.'

And then he turned and left, and everyone was too busy to notice that the smile I had

32

been wearing was now gone, replaced with a look of worry. I was so concerned that I had just made an enemy of the nastiest elf in Elfhelm that, for the rest of the evening, I completely forgot I was due to start my new school the very next day.

My First Year at Elf School

Elves were small but elf children were *smaller*. Even though I was technically a child I was quite tall by human-child standards, so I was *very* tall by elf-child standards.

I was always bumping my head on the school doorways, I could hardly squeeze my legs under the desk, and the seat of the chair seemed to be on the floor. The notepads and the crayons were too small. And the toilets – well, the toilets were just ridiculous.

But I did like it that all the classes had names. There was Frost Class and Gingerbread Class and Sleigh Bell Class, and the oldest elves were in Mistletoe Class. I was in Snowball Class.

I sat next to a smiley elf girl called Twinkle who was good at everything. All the elves were good at everything, but Twinkle especially. The reason Twinkle was so good at everything was because, even though she was a child, she was actually three hundred and seventy-two years old.

'Three hundred and seventy-two and a half, actually,' she told me on the first day. 'I know that might sound confusing, but what happens to elves is that we grow older and older, and then we stop growing old the moment we reach our perfect age, the age at which we truly know ourselves and will be happy for ever. Most elves generally don't find out who they are – what makes them happy, what they want to do – until they are quite old.'

I knew this already. For instance, I knew Father Topo was ninety-nine before he stopped ageing. Father Christmas – who is not technically an elf but a drimwicked human – stopped ageing somewhere in his sixties, when he discovered his destiny. But some such as Twinkle find out when they are very young. So Twinkle was eleven and three hundred and seventy-two (and a half) all at the same time.

There were about twenty of us in Snowball Class. As well as Twinkle there was also a tiny but extremely enthusiastic elf called Shortcrust, who was the junior spickle-dance champion, and Snowflake, who was a bit annoying and always laughed at me whenever I made a mistake, which was quite often.

We had different teachers for different subjects but our form teacher was Mother Jingle. She always looked at me with kind eyes, but I couldn't help thinking she thought I was a big waste of space.

It was she who told me, in my first week, that I wasn't ready for sleighcraft lessons just yet.

I felt anger boil inside me. It was an anger I hadn't really felt since the workhouse, and

Mr Jeremiah Creeper. 'But I've flown a sleigh before! I flew Father Christmas's sleigh! The biggest sleigh there is!'

She shook her head. 'I'm sorry, but when people arrive at this school, they have to wait six months before they are allowed to start flying sleighs. Those are Kip's rules, I'm afraid.'

'But most people who start at this school are five years old. I'm eleven.'

'You have lived for eleven years *as a human*, which is different. Humans aren't made for flying sleighs.'

And that was the end of it. I had to wait. And in the meantime I had to get on with all the other lessons.

There was maths, with Pi, which was really tricky. You see, elf mathematics is very different to human mathematics. In elf mathematics the best answer isn't the right one, it's the most interesting.

'Amelia, what is two plus two?' Pi would ask.

'Four,' I would say.

And the whole class would burst out laughing. Apart from Twinkle.

'Twinkle, tell Amelia the answer.'

And Twinkle would sit up straight and say, 'Snow.'

'Yes,' said Pi. 'Two plus two is snow. Or you could have said feather duvet.'

And then Twinkle would look at me and apologise for being right, which made it worse.

The other subjects were equally tricky.

There was Writing, Singing (my voice wasn't cheerful enough), Laughing Even When Times Are Tough (a *very* difficult lesson), Joke Making, Christmas Studies, Spickle Dancing (a disaster), Practical Drimwickery (even more of a disaster, obviously), Gingerbread, General Happiness and Geography.

Columbus – the geography teacher I had met along with Pi that day in the sweet shop – was a lovely elf, and I had high hopes for his lessons. They sounded quite ordinary and human, but of course they weren't. Elf geography was as crazy as all the other subjects. The whole of the globe, south of Very Big Mountain, was simply called 'the Human World'. It didn't matter if it was Finland or Britain or America or China, it was absolutely all the same to elves, and they left it up to Father Christmas – and now Mother Christmas – to plan which route Father Christmas should travel every year.

Everything this side of the mountain, on the other hand, was studied in great detail. These were called the Magic Places. And they included the Elf Territory (which was made up of Elfhelm, and the Wooded Hills, which was more accurately *pixie* territory, but apparently pixies were terrible at geography and didn't care very much about the names of things and so none of them objected). The other Magic Places were Troll Valley, the Ice Plains (where Tomtegubbs could often be found), the Hulderlands (home to the Hulder-folk) and the Land of Hills and Holes.

Days and weeks and months went by. Father Christmas came home late a lot of the time, because this was the busiest year for the workshop ever. Mary was also very busy, as she was in charge of Christmas route planning. She had also begun to take drimwickery classes, so she could unleash her magic, but she was finding it quite difficult. Anyway, they both became very preoccupied and I didn't want to bother them with my problems, so I just whispered my complaints to Captain Soot, who always purred some comfort.

I've always been the kind of person who could look after herself. I've always had to, really. And, in fact, for most of the year I made the most of it. And a lot of the time I had fun. A lot of fun. Living in Elfhelm was still a lot better than being an orphan in London.

I often went to Twinkle's house to play elf tennis, which is exactly like normal tennis but with an imaginary ball rather than a real one. This was one elf sport I was good at, and I wished we could have played it at school. Then I would go home and read or bounce on the trampoline or read *while* bouncing on the trampoline.

Even my lessons weren't all bad. Twinkle was fun to sit next to and always told great jokes, and Shortcrust would often entertain us with his spickle dancing at playtime. And even on bad days I kept on saying to myself that things would be much better when the sleighcraft lessons happened. But six months went by. Then seven. Then eight. And soon it was December, and it seemed that I might never be allowed to take part in a sleighcraft lesson and would always have to stay by myself in an empty classroom, staring out of the window at the other pupils in my class flying past in sleighs.

It was getting quite close to Christmas when I first spoke to Mary and Father Christmas about it. It was the day I first heard mention of the Land of Hills and Holes.

'Where is it?' I asked Columbus.

'Very far away. The furthest away it is possible to be, within the Magic Places. About a hundred miles east of Troll Valley.'

'And who lives there?'

The whole class knew the answer, but instead of giggling at me like they normally did they all went very quiet.

'Some rather dangerous creatures.'

'What?'

'*Rabbits.*'

It was then my turn to laugh. 'Rabbits? Rabbits aren't dangerous.'

Columbus nodded wisely. 'I see. You are thinking about the kind of rabbits you find in the Human World. Little cute hoppy things with big ears. Hop, hop, hop! Father Christmas told me about them. But no, these rabbits are very different. These rabbits are bigger. They stand on their hind legs. And they are' – he took a moment, swallowed – '*deadly.*'

'Deadly?' I couldn't help but smile. It sounded so ridiculous.

'He's serious,' whispered Twinkle.

'Yes,' said Columbus, whose eyebrows lowered in disapproval. 'And it's no laughing matter . . . Who can tell Amelia about the rabbits who live in the Land of Hills and Holes?'

Snowflake was first with her hand up.

'Yes, Snowflake?'

'Their ruler is the Easter Bunny.'

I stifled a giggle.

'Correct,' said Columbus. 'Their ruler is the Easter Bunny. Everyone knows that. Well, everyone apart from Amelia. Now, anything else?'

Twinkle, inevitably, put up her hand. 'They have a very big army. There are thousands of them. Tens of thousands. And hundreds of years ago they had battles with trolls and elves. There were the Troll Wars, which they won, and before that, when elves used to live throughout the whole of the Magic Lands, the Rabbit Army fought them and beat them, and took the Land of Hills and Holes for themselves.'

Columbus, as always, looked very pleased with Twinkle. 'Exactly. In the very olden days, when the rabbits lived in warrens below the ground, the elves and rabbits lived quite peacefully together. But then one day, when the Easter Bunny took over the army, he had a different idea. He wanted everyone to know about rabbits. Yes, they still kept their warrens to sleep and work in, but they no longer wanted to be scared or to hide away. Especially in summer. They liked the light. They liked the warmth. They wanted to be running free. They wanted to go wherever. Which would have been fine, but they didn't want anyone but rabbits around them either. They forced the elves out. Well, those elves who made it out alive – which wasn't many of them.'

'Oh no,' I said, 'how terrible.'

Columbus sighed. 'Well, it was a very long

time ago. And the rabbits keep themselves to themselves and so do we. So there is nothing to worry about.'

'How can you be sure?' I asked him.

'Because he's the teacher!' said Twinkle. Everyone laughed as if I was stupid. Still, my head was full of questions and the questions had nowhere to go except out of my mouth.

'Why is he called the Easter Bunny?' I asked.

Columbus again pointed at Twinkle. 'Twinkle, explain why the Easter Bunny is called the Easter Bunny.'

Twinkle took a very deep breath and sat up super-straight. 'He is called the Easter Bunny because it was Easter when they came out of their burrows. Easter is when things get warmer and lighter, and it was also when the first and last battle between the elves and the rabbits happened.'

'Oh, so what was the Easter Bunny called before?'

'Seven-four-nine,' said Columbus. 'Rabbits tend to call themselves numbers rather than names. They are a very mathematical species.'

'Right,' I said, 'I see.' But I didn't really. There were still questions inside my head. For instance: if the Easter Bunny and his Rabbit Army wanted to be everywhere, why didn't they ever want to be in Elfhelm? Was the threat from the rabbits over? Was the Easter Bunny even still alive?

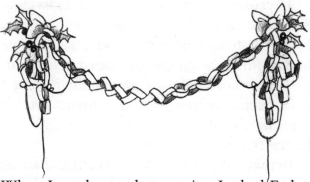

When I got home that evening I asked Father Christmas about the Easter Bunny.

'Oh,' he said, as we made paper chains, 'the Rabbit War was way before I arrived here. Way before I was even born. There are some very, very old elves who remember what life was like in the Land of Hills and Holes. Father Topo is one of them. He was six at the time, when the elves had to retreat here. He said it wasn't so special and most elves didn't really miss it. It was a very flat place. No woods. No hills. Nothing except rabbit holes . . .'

An hour later, we were around the table, eating cherry pie.

I was still curious about rabbits. 'If it's so boring, how do we know the rabbits won't come here and take Elfhelm too?'

Father Christmas smiled that reassuring smile of his. His eyes twinkled. 'Because it was three hundred years ago. And in all that time there hasn't been so much as a single bunny hop near Elfhelm. Whatever the rabbits are up to, they are up to it a long way away, and so there is no need to worry about anything at all. Nothing's changed.'

That reassured me. But my face must have still looked glum, because Mary said, 'What's the matter, sweetheart?'

I sighed. I had always thought it best not to complain too much about life here, as there was no doubt that it was a lot better than life in Creeper's Workhouse in London. But Mary's stare was the kind of stare that made you have to tell the truth, so I came straight out with it.

'School,' I said. 'School's the matter.'

Mary's head tilted in sympathy. 'What's wrong at school?'

'Everything,' I said. 'All year it's been a bit tricky. I'm just not good at elf subjects. They don't make any sense to me. And I'll *never* get the hang of elf mathematics . . .'

Father Christmas nodded. 'Ah, yes. Elf mathematics does take some getting used to. I couldn't believe it when I learned that the five times table here is an actual table – made of wood, with five legs. And long division is just normal division that you write down *really* slowly. But don't worry. Everyone finds it hard.'

'But they don't,' I said, picturing in my mind Twinkle's hand shooting up faster than a star. 'And it's not just maths either. I find it all hard. I am the least cheerful singer the school has ever known, even when I really try. And Laughing Even When Times Are Tough is a really stupid subject to begin with. I mean, why *should* people laugh when times are tough? If times are tough, I think it is perfectly normal *not* to smile. You shouldn't have to smile at *everything*, should you?'

'Oh dear,' said Father Christmas. 'I daren't ask about the spickle dancing.'

'It's terrible. Humans just aren't made for spickle dancing.'

'Tell me about it,' said Mary.

'I mean, I'm fine with the footwork but it's the hovering in the air. That's just impossible.'

Father Christmas winced as if a firework had just gone off. 'Don't say that word.'

I must have been in a very bad mood because all of a sudden I was saying it, over and over. 'Impossible. Impossible. Impossible. Impossible.'

'Amelia,' said Mary, 'you know there is no swearing in the house.'

'But impossible shouldn't even *be* a swear

word. Some things simply are impossible. For an ordinary normal human being spickle dancing simply *is* impossible. And Practical Drimwickery is impossible. And on some Monday mornings even Happiness is impossible.'

'Happiness is never impossible,' said Father Christmas. 'Nothing is impossible. An impossibility is just a—'

'I know. I know. An impossibility is just a possibility you don't understand yet. I have heard it a hundred times. But what about walking on the ceiling? That's impossible. What about flying to the stars? That's impossible.'

'It isn't, actually,' muttered Father Christmas. 'It isn't *impossible*. It's just not the right thing to do. And that's a very big difference.'

'Listen,' said Mary. 'I know how difficult it is, fitting in. I've been taking drimwickery classes for months and I'm getting nowhere, but I'm going to keep trying. There must be some subjects you enjoy?'

I thought. Captain Soot rubbed his head against my leg, as if to comfort me.

'Yes, there is one. Writing. I like writing. I like it a lot. When I write, I feel free.'

'Well, there you go. That's good,' said Father Christmas. 'And what about sleigh riding. You like sleigh riding, surely? You are *brilliant* at sleigh riding.'

And then I told them what I had been too ashamed to tell them. 'They don't let me do that.'

'What?' asked Mary and Father Christmas both at once.

'Because this is my first year at the school. And because I am a human. They said I had to wait six months until I could start flying sleighs. Nearly a year now has passed. But it's okay. They might be right. Maybe Father Vodol was right, at your wedding. Maybe I don't belong here.'

'What a load of old butterscotch!' said Mary, whose cheeks were even redder than usual. 'You belong here as much as I do. Or as much as anyone, in fact. The likes of us, Amelia, were always made to feel like we were a burden. Send us off to the workhouse! Out of sight! But you are a good person, Amelia, and goodness belongs anywhere in this world. You remember that!'

'Mary's right,' agreed Father Christmas. 'And Father Vodol is a hateful elf who should be ignored. You have just as much right to fly a sleigh as any elf child has. Don't worry! I'll have a word with the school. And with Kip at the School of Sleighcraft. I'll put an end to this silliness. But only on one condition . . .'

'What's that?' I asked.

'That you try not to say the word *impossible* in this house again.'

I laughed. Mary laughed. Even Captain Soot seemed to laugh. 'All right. It's a deal.'

The Sleigh Ride

I t happened.

Father Christmas must have said something.

Because the following Monday afternoon – a week before Christmas – I was finally allowed to take part in the sleigh-riding lesson. And I was, I have to tell you, very, very excited. I hardly slept all weekend. And when I woke up that Monday morning Father Christmas recommended I bounce on the trampoline for 'at least half an hour' to keep my excitement under control. This was, you see, my one chance of fitting in. It was the one elfish thing I knew I could do.

The teacher, Kip, was a good friend of Father Christmas. When Kip was five years old, Father Christmas had saved his life. Once, when I asked Father Christmas how he saved his life, he shook his head and said, 'Some things are best forgotten.' Kip didn't like talking at all, unless it was about sleighs, so that was all I knew.

So there we were, in the School of Sleighcraft on the Main Path. All the red-and-white learner sleighs were lined up. They were small, far smaller than Father Christmas's sleigh, and only needed one reindeer to pull them.

'Shortcrust, take Prancer,' said Kip, pointing at the closest sleigh.

Shortcrust yelped, 'Yay!'

'Twinkle, you have Dasher.'

'Yes, Mr Kip,' said Twinkle.

'Snowflake, you're on Comet.'

This went on until all the elves were given a sleigh to ride.

I waved at Kip. He pretended not to see. 'Can't I ride a sleigh?' I said.

Kip's eyes narrowed. Underneath his heavy fringe he looked at me with suspicion. 'Humans shouldn't fly sleighs.'

I got the feeling that Kip didn't like humans very much.

'Father Christmas is a human.'

Kip shook his head. 'Father Christmas is not an *ordinary* human. Father Christmas is a human who has been drimwicked.'

I remembered how people used to think I was too young to sweep chimneys, when Ma was ill and I used to go to her customers' houses. I proved them wrong, and I would prove Kip wrong. I stayed strong.

'I can fly a sleigh,' I said. 'That's why I'm here.'

I watched as Twinkle and Dasher trotted into place on the runway, shortly followed by Shortcrust and Prancer and all the other elves.

I had that horribly familiar feeling of being left out. Tears welled in my eyes.

'Okay, okay,' said Kip. 'I suppose we'd better find a sleigh then.'

I smiled. 'Thanks, Mr Kip.'

'Just do everything I say. Okay?'

'Yes, yes, I promise.' I stared around the yard. All the sleighs and reindeer were already taken. Then I spotted, in the corner of the yard, a small, empty, shiny white sleigh attached to Blitzen, Father Christmas's reindeer. It was the sleigh I had seen months ago, the day we had visited Bonbon's sweet shop. The gleaming, beautiful, expensive one.

'There,' I said, pointing to it. 'That one.'

'But that's a Blizzard 360,' said Kip, looking very worried indeed.

'So?'

'That's my newest sleigh. It's worth a thousand chocolate coins.'

He looked around, desperately trying to find

another sleigh to put me in, but they all had elves sitting inside, ready for take-off.

Kip looked up at me and rolled his eyes. 'Okay then. You *can* fly the Blizzard 360. But you must be very careful. Very, very careful. Very, very, very, very, very careful. Do you understand?'

'Yes. Very, very, very, very, very careful. Five verys. Got it.'

So he took me over and I climbed into the sleigh. The seat felt comfortable and luxurious.

Kip pointed to the dashboard. The tips of his elf fingers stuck out of his fingerless gloves. The dashboard was like a smaller version of the one in Father Christmas's sleigh.

'There's your altitude gauge and that's the Barometer of Hope – which needs to stay with the arrow pointing there – and you need to check that the hope converter sign keeps glowing green the whole time. The compass is right there in the centre. The dial for the propulsion unit needs to be between eighty and a hundred, ideally, but turn it up to one hundred and fifty for take-off, and slow down to sixty when you are ready to land. And the reins are the best in existence, so you only need to be gentle with them when steering. Light tugs for left or right. Pull low to descend. Three tugs for a sharp turn. Understand?'

I nodded. 'Understood.' I stared at the Barometer of Hope. It worked by picking up on all the hope particles in the air. And there was a lot of hope in the air, these days, since Elfhelm had made peace with the trolls.

Kip grumbled something under his breath and left me to it. He went to the front of the yard, beside the runway, and started shouting instructions to everyone.

'Right, everyone, in a minute, when I say your name, you will tug the reins five times and the reindeer will start to gallop as fast as it can along the runway.'

The runway was just like every other piece of snow-covered ground in Elfhelm. And it wasn't very long. You had to fly into the air quite quickly or you would end up crashing into the school.

'You will then gently rise into the air,' said Kip. 'Lean back in your seat and don't let go of the reins. Once you are airborne it is simple. A gentle pull of the reins to the right to move right and left for left. Do you understand?'

'Yes,' said all the elves eagerly.

'Amelia,' shouted Kip, 'do you hear me?'

I nodded.

'Right, good. So, now, there is one big rule,' said Kip. 'When you are flying, make sure you only fly above Elfhelm in circles. Do not go near Very Big Mountain and you must never head over the Wooded Hills. This is very important.'

I nodded and then I heard a soft miaowing. I looked down and saw Captain Soot's green eyes staring up at me. I saw his little footsteps in the deep snow. I couldn't believe it.

'*I told you to stay in the house,*' I whispered. '*Go back home. You shouldn't be here. Cats aren't allowed.*'

Captain Soot ignored me and jumped into the sleigh.

'*No! Get out of here. Get out. Go home. You can't be here, Captain, you'll get me into—*'

'Is anything the matter, Amelia?' Kip had noticed I was acting a bit strange, and now all the elves were staring straight at me.

There was no way I was going to tell them the truth. I'd be in trouble and Kip would use it as an excuse to make me miss the lesson and then I would be made to feel even more like a tall weird human who was rubbish at everything. This was my one chance to show them there was one thing I wasn't rubbish at – sleigh riding.

'No, nothing's the matter. Nothing at all.'

Kip stared at me suspiciously for a little longer.

'Good. Then get hold of your reins. We are about to start.'

There was no feeling like it.

Being up in the sky, with Elfhelm far below, the air blasting into my face, and Blitzen galloping in front, pulling the sleigh, his hooves landing on nothing at all.

Everything was going perfectly well. Kip was far below with a large red-and-white striped shouting cone – as elves called it – barking up instructions.

'Very good, Shortcrust! Tighter on the reins, Twinkle! Slow down, Snowflake! That's it, Amelia! Well done!'

I couldn't believe it. This was amazing. Kip had given me a compliment. He thought I was doing well. And that was because I *was* doing well, and now all the elves on their sleighs were turning to have a look at me as we soared in circuits in the sky.

I had good control of the reins. Blitzen was relaxed and galloping without much effort. The Barometer of Hope was holding steady around the 'Really Quite Hopeful' mark.

I looked down below and saw the school, and the Toy Workshop, and the village hall. I think I saw Father Christmas and Mary, holding hands, as they walked along the Street of Seven Curves.

I kept on.

'Good boy, Blitzen,' I said. 'Keep going.'

'One more time around!' Kip shouted. 'Then everyone is going to land on the runway. Pull the reins low, please. One by one. Starting with Shortcrust and Dancer . . . Okay? One more time around!'

It was going so well I was smiling – laughing almost. My life had once been a miserable human one, trapped in a workhouse from morning until night, but here I was in a magical land full of elves and wonder and *flying a sleigh*. Yes, so I had found some of the subjects at school a bit hard, but things were going to get better now.

'Wow!' said Snowflake, as Blitzen and I overtook him. 'You're amazing!'

And then Dasher galloped through the air beside me, as fast as ever, with Snowflake standing up in her sleigh behind. 'Wow, Amelia!' she said. 'It looks like you've found your subject!'

And as the wind sped through my hair I couldn't stop myself shouting into the wind, 'THIS IS BRILLIANT! LIFE IS BRILLIANT! WOO HOO!' And this was many, many years before anyone had said 'woo hoo'. I am quite sure I invented it. But, honestly, all I can say is, in that moment everything seemed *just right*. Perfect, in fact.

But then . . .

Captain Soot, who had been lying snugly beside my feet, jumped onto my lap.

'No, Captain, keep down. It's dangerous up here. We're very high up.'

But Captain Soot had never been very good at following instructions. He was a cat, after all.

I held the reins with one hand and tried to pick up Captain Soot with the other, to place him back down at my feet. Just as I tried to scoop up Captain Soot he jumped onto the front of the sleigh, above the dashboard. And then he began to slide downwards.

'Oh no!'

Captain Soot's sharp claws scratched down the front of the Blizzard 360.

I let go of the reins, stood up and leant forward to grab him. The sleigh began to lose direction a little.

'Amelia! What are you doing?' shouted Snowflake from behind me.

There was no time to answer. Captain Soot's eyes were wide with fear. I quickly grabbed hold of him, but awkwardly as he was so far forwards.

'It's all right, Captain. I've got you.'

But he wasn't comforted. The cold wind was blasting so fast over him he panicked even more. Then, something terrible happened.

Captain Soot, out of sheer fright, nearly half a mile high in the air, jumped out of my arms.

The Cat and the Reindeer

'No!' I screamed.

The thing is it would have been fine if Captain Soot had jumped backwards into the sleigh. But he didn't. He jumped in the opposite direction. Forwards. *Out* of the sleigh. And when I looked over the side of the sleigh I couldn't see him. He was nowhere.

And then I spotted him.

Captain Soot had landed on Blitzen's back, where he was now clinging on for his life. Blitzen turned his head to see the black furry creature digging its claws into his fur and his eyes widened in horror. He wriggled to try to shake the cat off. I didn't see much after that because I was flung back, falling into the sleigh and unable to stand up because it was wobbling so much. I tried to catch hold of the reins but the sleigh was tilting so fast – up and down and side to side.

'Blitzen! Calm down! Blitzen! It's all right! It's just a cat! Blitzen! BLITZAAAAAAAAAA-AAAAAAAGHHH!'

Blitzen was now charging at full speed, overtaking even Dasher, and leaving all the other elves and reindeer far behind in the sky.

I could just about hear Kip's voice far away, bellowing, 'Amelia! Amelia! What are you doing? Come back here this instant! Get control of your reindeer now! Amelia! This is your final . . .'

I could no longer hear Kip. Blitzen was galloping at breakneck speed. The sleigh was now a little bit steadier because Blitzen was travelling in one direction incredibly fast.

Somehow, with great effort, I managed to get to my feet. Gripping both sides of the sleigh, I looked over and realised to my horror that we were heading straight for the place we were told to avoid – the Wooded Hills.

I looked behind and could hardly see the other sleighs. Elfhelm was like a little colourful toy village disappearing into the distance.

'Oh no, oh no, oh no.'

I leaned over the side, desperately trying to grasp hold of the leather reins that were whipping about like over-excited snakes.

'Oh no, oh no, oh no, oh no, oh no, oh no, oh no.'

It was useless. I couldn't grab them. I saw Captain Soot clawing his way over Blitzen's back, towards his neck.

'No, Captain! No. This way. Come to me. Come on. Please, Captain. Please!'

It was no good saying 'please' to a cat. It was no good saying anything to a cat, really. A cat is a cat. But what else could I do?

It seemed that Blitzen was almost trying to gallop away from Captain Soot. Which was quite a difficult thing to do, as Captain Soot was attached to his back.

I looked down at the ground. We were very high. Higher than the trees that we were flying over. And very far away from Elfhelm, now. In fact, it was nowhere to be seen. We were probably miles away.

'Oh no, oh no, oh no, oh no, oh no, oh no, oh no, oh no, oh no, oh no, oh no, oh no.'

'Blitzen!' I shouted one last time at the crazed reindeer. 'It's all right. It's all right. It's . . .'

I had an idea.

It was a totally stupid idea, but it was the only one I had.

I had to get control of Blitzen. And I couldn't get control of him from the sleigh. That was absolutely impossible now that I didn't have the reins.

No. The only way I could get control of Blitzen, and the reins, and grab hold of Captain Soot, was to jump from the sleigh onto the reindeer's back.

So I reached the front of the sleigh and put my left foot on the dashboard, right on top of the Barometer of Hope, which was now at its lowest setting of all: 'Actually Not Much Hope At All'. Then I held on to the small front rail just above the dashboard as I brought my other foot up.

The cold wind was blasting my face with a ferocious force, whipping my hair back in a straight line behind me.

'All right,' I told myself. 'Come on, Amelia. You can do this. Captain Soot did it. But Captain Soot is a cat, and a cat who is very good at jumping and also very good at landing. Oh, come on. Stop arguing with yourself. Just do it. JUST DO IT!'

I did it.

I jumped through the air and landed with a bump just above Blitzen's bottom. This caused the reindeer to buck in the air like a wild bull, as he tried to fling me off.

'Blitzen!' I said, as my face smashed into his back. 'Blitzen, what are you doing? It's me, Amelia!'

And it was then that he seemed to understand, and he became a little less wild and crazy, and at last his air gallop began to slow to a canter.

'Good boy, Blitzen. Good boy.'

Now I had a choice. I could either reach for Captain Soot or grab hold of the reins.

In that moment, I went for the reins.

It was the wrong choice.

You see, the moment I had hold of the reins was also the moment Captain Soot lost his grip.

'Oh no!'

I quickly reached out to catch Captain Soot but only managed to touch the white tip of his tail before he began to fall, fast through the air, towards the trees below.

'Captaaaain!'

I got a tight hold of the reins, and pulled them low, which I knew – as Kip had told me – was the way to make a reindeer start to descend and prepare for landing.

'Low, Blitzen! Low! Low! Low!'

I think Blitzen knew what he had done. I don't think until that moment he realised there had been a cat on his back. He had just known there was *something* on him and he hadn't liked it one little bit. But now he seemed to understand that it wasn't just anything. He knew it was my cat and that it was important to me, and that it was probably therefore important to Father Christmas, and if there was one thing a reindeer – especially Blitzen – hated more than anything, it was upsetting

Father Christmas. So Blitzen was now diving fast through the air, faster than gravity, towards Captain Soot.

The sleigh was slowing us down so I unclipped the straps that attached it to the reindeer and it went whizzing off behind us.

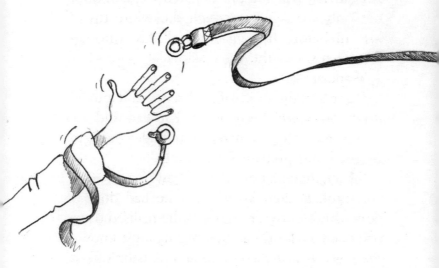

Then I saw him.

A tiny black speck, getting bigger as we sped towards him, faster than he was falling.

He was level with the top tips of the highest spruce trees on the hills. But the dark green branches wouldn't slow or cushion his descent as he was too far away, directly between the trees.

'Faster, Blitzen! Fast as you can! As fast as magic!'

I wished Father Christmas was there. If Father Christmas had been there, he would have been able to do some drimwickery and stop time. But then, if Father Christmas had been there none of this would have happened in the first place.

Captain Soot.

He was right there.

I could see him, spinning wildly through the air, his tail flapping like a loose rein.

I reached my arms low and grabbed Captain Soot before he hit the ground as Blitzen swooped through the air in a U-shape, jerking fast upwards so we didn't all crash.

'It's all right, Captain! I've got you! You're safe now! We're alive! Somehow we're alive!'

The relief flooded through me like warm milk. And just as Blitzen was slowing to make a gentle landing on the forest floor, there was an incredibly loud noise behind us which broke our happiness.

Smash!

I turned to see the sleigh, the gleaming Blizzard 360, smashed into a smoking pile of rubble on the forest floor.

'OH NO.'

The Hole

We landed, and as I held on to Captain Soot I climbed off Blitzen.

When I was safely on the ground, I patted the reindeer. 'I'm sorry, Blitzen. Captain Soot was just scared. Are you all right?'

Blitzen looked at Captain Soot in my arms and made a funny kind of truffling sound.

'I'll take that as a yes. Come on, we had better find the sleigh and inspect the damage.'

We walked through the trees. I could feel Captain Soot's heart beating incredibly fast so, although I was cross with him for nearly killing us all, I gave him a little kiss on his head and stroked him.

I heard something fluttering over my head and looked up to see a boy pixie with shimmering silvery see-through wings smiling at me mischievously. He darted down like a bird towards me and whispered in my ear.

'Once upon a time, there was a paper

bird . . .' he said, with a voice as smooth as silk. 'Flying out of a hole and into the light . . .'

'Paper bird?'

'Birds, I should have said. Paper birds, yes. Or words. Please may I have some words?'

Then the boy pixie giggled.

'Words?'

'Yes, words. I like words. Like burrow. That is a good word.'

'I know lots of words,' I told him as I stopped walking and tugged Blitzen's reins for him to do the same. I looked at the pixie. His wings shone like glass, and the sun glinted off them. 'But I am just going over to see my sleigh.'

The pixie flew around me and then ended up hovering in exactly the same spot. There were several species of pixie who lived in the Wooded Hills, but this particular type was a Flying Story Pixie. I had seen a whole bunch of them before, the night I first met Father Christmas. Flying Story Pixies, as their name suggested, were pixies who flew around the forest telling stories to other pixies and to anyone else they would come by.

They fed on words the way bears feed on honey and were always on the hunt for new ones, exotic words, with which to spice up their stories.

'*But I am just going over to see my sleigh,*' the Flying Story Pixie repeated, screwing his little nose up as if tasting something he didn't like. He tried it again. '*But I am just going over to see my sleigh.* I must say that these are very ordinary words you have given me.'

'I'm sorry but I just had a bit of a disaster.'

'*I'm sorry but I just had a bit of a disaster.* Hmmm. Yes, that's better. *Disaster* is a good word. It's not as good as catastrophe. Or calamity. Or impossible. Which is an elf swear word. I love saying it, especially to elves. Impossible. Impossible. They get so annoyed.'

'Listen, I'm really enjoying this conversation but the thing is I really need to go and see my sleigh.'

The Flying Story Pixie smiled and clapped his hands. 'Yes. That is the perfect example of impossible. Because, let's face it, it *is* impossible. I just flew over the sleigh and I can tell you that it is very broken indeed.'

'Well, anyway, I'd better go and see.'

I walked away.

The pixie looked sad. 'Please . . . please just give me one word that I have never heard before.'

I tried to think. I realised he wasn't going to fly away and leave me alone until I actually gave him a new word.

He looked at Captain Soot in my arms. 'What is that?' he asked.

Captain Soot hissed up at him.

'This is a cat.'

'Cat? Cat? Cat! That is a brilliant word. Cat. Cat. Thank you very much. I have never heard that word before. I have never seen a cat before.'

'I don't think you get many of them around here,' I said as I placed Captain Soot on the ground. 'Anyway, it was good to talk. Bye.'

The pixie took the hint and darted away through the trees. Blitzen, Captain Soot and I walked over to the sleigh. Or what was left of the sleigh.

The pixie had been right.

It really was in a state.

'This can't be happening,' I said.

The dashboard was smashed. There was a crack right through the Barometer of Hope and the dial was spinning round and round. Springs were sticking out of everywhere. The seat had become totally detached and was lying half out of the sleigh. The main body had a giant crack running all the way through it. The whole thing was almost split in two. This was a disaster. Only a few minutes ago I had been having the absolute time of my life and now I felt sick.

'Oh, Blitzen, what are we going to do?'

Blitzen didn't know. He lowered his head to the ground and made the truffling sound again, but this time it sounded worried.

I looked around at the forest. The trees were tall and dark. I had absolutely no idea where we were. Pretty soon it was going to be evening. Then we'd be in real trouble. But if I arrived in Elfhelm without the sleigh I'd be in real trouble too.

'All right, Blitzen. There's only one thing we can do. I'll attach the harness back on you and then we'll have to walk back as you pull the sleigh. No galloping. No flying. We don't want to do any more damage.'

I almost cried when I said that. After all, it didn't look like it was actually possible to do any more damage to the sleigh.

So I strapped the sleigh harness onto Blitzen and then I picked up Captain Soot, who was shaking with cold, and we began to walk.

We walked and walked and walked. I heard distant birdsong and the occasional flutter of a pixie up ahead and saw bright red toadstools growing out of the ground. The cool air smelt of pine. The trees seemed to reach the sky. Their branches blocked out the sun. Everywhere was so thick with shade that the shadows appeared as real and solid as the trees that caused them. And it felt like the forest went on for ever.

But that wasn't the main thing that worried me. The thing that worried me was how weird it was here. I began to hear a noise. A kind of humming. The humming got louder and louder. I wondered where it was coming from. And then I realised it was coming from *all around*. There were flowers, tall turquoise flowers, suddenly everywhere. And when I bent down to have a look at them the humming grew louder still. It was a deep, quite scary humming noise. The closer I got to them, the louder the flowers became.

'There once was a flower,' said a voice from above, 'that hummed every hour.'

I looked up.

A female Flying Story Pixie was sitting in a tree, eating berries.

Then I turned back to the turquoise flower I was closest to.

'And once a girl sniffed it like a rose. And it spat on her – right on her nose.' She sighed. 'They are Spitting Flowers. If you get too close they will—'

And just at that minute the flower I was closest to spat a horrible, stinking bright blue spray of flower juice on my face.

'Ah, I love a story with a happy ending,' laughed the Flying Story Pixie as she fluttered away. 'You have ten seconds before it kills you.'

'What?'

'Don't worry! I was joking. It's actually five seconds.'

Frantically I wiped the spray off my face and from Captain Soot's fur with my sleeve. I looked into Captain Soot's eyes and whispered, 'Sorry, Captain, I'm so sorry, you've been the best cat ever.' And I waited to die. But five seconds passed and then ten seconds and then a minute and I was still breathing. And so was Captain Soot. I hugged him close. 'Yes!' I said, 'we're alive, we're alive.' Captain Soot miaowed, as if it was no big deal, and we carried on walking.

There were other strange things in the forest. In fact, there were *only* strange things. There was a two-headed squirrel. We saw a group of miniature four-eyed bears, as small as mice, who tried to climb up Blitzen's legs to attack him. And then we met the weirdest thing of all. At first it looked like a perfectly ordinary pine tree, but the bark on the trunk blinked open a pair of eyes. Then, below them a hole opened into a mouth.

'You are lost, aren't you?' it said.

I staggered back in shock, clutching Captain Soot. 'You're a talking tree.'

'Yes, well observed. I'm the Talking Tree,' the tree said with a sigh. 'But you *are* lost, aren't you?'

'How did you know that?'

'Everyone is lost here.'

'Yes, well, we're not really lost. We know where we are going. We just don't entirely know how to get there.'

'That,' said the tree, who seemed an arrogant kind of tree, 'is the definition of lost.'

'Well, I suppose so, but there's no need to be so . . . Okay, yes, I need to get back home.'

The tree smiled. It was a strange smile, which was really the only kind of smile trees knew

how to do. '*Home is not a place, as every tree knows. You take home with you, wherever you go.*'

'That's a nice riddle. Thanks. But I really need to get to Elfhelm.'

The tree exhaled. It was taking its time. Talking very slowly. 'You are a very odd-looking elf.'

'I'm not an elf.'

'Then why do you want to go to Elfhelm?'

'Because I live there.'

'Oh, and I'm a daisy.'

'No, really, I live there. Please, do you know the way?'

Blitzen was nudging my shoulder, trying to tell me something, but I wasn't paying attention. Or at least I wasn't until I felt something twist around my ankle. I looked down and could hardly believe my eyes. A root from the tree had come out of the ground and was coiling around my leg. And now it was trying to drag me towards the mouth of the tree.

'So sorry,' said the tree. 'It's really nothing personal.'

Blitzen bit hard into the root that had hold of me. The root quickly uncoiled, and I stepped back as the tree let out a howl of pain.

We hurried away from the Talking Tree, and carried on walking. I wanted desperately to be out of the forest, even though I knew Kip was going to be furious about the sleigh.

We walked another mile or so, past more Spitting Flowers, and stones covered in purple moss, but no more Talking Trees.

I kicked a pine cone and saw it disappear into something very strange that filled the forest path ahead of us.

A hole.

A crooked dark circle, blacker than the shadows, in the ground.

I got closer to it as Blitzen dragged the sleigh around it. I stood right next to the edge and stared down. The hole was probably as wide as the sleigh itself. Maybe a bit wider.

It was dark down there. It reminded me of the darkness of chimneys. I wondered why there would be a big hole in the middle of a forest. Maybe it was the trolls. Or maybe it was rabbits. It looked too big to have been created by a rabbit, but then I remembered Columbus's geography lesson where he had talked about the Easter Bunny and the large rabbits in the Land of Hills and Holes. But it was meant to be a very long way away. Maybe

it was created by another creature. A creature I had never heard of. It almost seemed to be made from the forest itself. From the weight of shadows. Whatever, it was quite scary being there. I leant over and thought I could see something in the dark. A fast-moving shadow.

I jumped back.

I hesitantly peeped over the edge again.

Nothing. Just darkness.

I stepped back and a twig snapped underneath my feet. I jumped and nearly dropped Captain Soot. 'Sorry, Captain. Come on, let's go,' I said.

We left the hole behind and headed through the forest, down a long wooded slope.

Captain Soot was fidgeting in my arms, looking this way and that.

'Calm down, Captain. It's all right. Surely we're not far off now.'

But he wasn't calming down.

His head was jerking to and fro, like a bird. He had spotted something on the ground. Before I had time to hold him tighter, he jumped out of my arms and darted beneath Blitzen's legs.

I ran after him, and soon I saw a small wooden cottage with yellow walls and a yellow roof. It was even smaller than an elf's house, and they are pretty small. My head was probably level with the chimney. Captain Soot was heading straight towards the house, and just as he was close to it, the door opened and he disappeared inside, fast as a bullet.

'Great,' I said to myself.

Turning around I saw that Blitzen was slowly dragging the sleigh towards me. It creaked and groaned as it travelled over the rough sloping ground.

'Okay, Blitzen, be careful. I've got to knock on this door and get Captain Soot back.'

So I went to the door and crouched a little because it was obviously a small door. I could hear noises inside and a voice saying, 'It's all right, Maarta. Mummy's here. Mummy's here.' And then I heard Captain Soot do a big miaow.

I knocked on the door three times.

I waited.

And *waited*.

Then . . .

The door opened and a girl pixie stuck her head out to stare up at me. She had big wide-apart eyes and clear skin and ears pointier than even the pointiest elf ears.

I recognised her instantly.

'Hello. It's the Truth Pixie, isn't it?'

The Truth Pixie nodded. 'Of course it is.

Why do you ask a question that isn't a question? You know who I am. You've met me twice. You're a human. You come from the human world. I was the first pixie you ever met. So don't put a question mark there. Just say, "Hello, Truth Pixie." Like that. Understand?'

'I understand.'

'Good. Now, have a good day.'

She shut the door in my face.

I knocked again.

Waited again.

And waited.

And waited.

She opened the door and looked extremely disappointed to see that it was still me.

'What is it this time? I thought we were done.'

'No. I hadn't even asked the thing I wanted to ask.'

'What was the thing you wanted to ask?'

'I wanted to ask if I could have my cat back.'

'Cat? What's a *cat*?'

'That,' I said, pointing to Captain Soot, who was lying contentedly on a yellow rug by the tiny fireplace, 'is a cat. *My* cat.'

'Oh, I thought it was a horse. I have heard about horses. Father Christmas once told me about horses. Four-legged handsome things without antlers, and I thought, ah, here is a four-legged handsome thing without antlers. It must be a horse. And for one minute I felt so happy, being a horse owner. Although, to be truthful, well I am always truthful I am a Truth Pixie after all, Maarta is not so happy.'

'Maarta?' I asked. 'Is that your—'

I was going to say 'daughter' but already the Truth Pixie was nodding her head with great enthusiasm and saying, 'Mouse. Yes, she is my mouse. She was out roaming in the forest as she always does and then suddenly I heard her

squeaking at the door and I opened it – the
door, not the mouse – and in came not only
Maarta but the horse as well.'

'Cat.'

'Cat. Exactly. And Maarta was so excited I
had to put her up on her shelf.'

The Truth Pixie opened the door wider for
me to see, and there she was, a little brown
mouse nibbling on a piece of cheese on the
shelf above the fireplace safely out of Captain
Soot's reach.

'Listen, Truth Pixie, my cat really shouldn't

be near your mouse. You see, unlike horses, cats like eating mice. And Captain Soot was obviously chasing after Maarta and that—'

'You are ugly,' said the Truth Pixie.

'What? That's *rude*.'

'I am sorry. I can't help it. I am the Truth Pixie. The truth is what I do. But it is nothing personal.'

'Well, it feels personal.'

'Why? I have now seen three humans and they are all hideous. Father Christmas and Mary and you. Out of those three I would probably say you are the least ugly. But that still makes you incredibly hideous to look at. It is your ears. They are so round. And your eyes. Human eyes are just too close together. They are ridiculous. And look how tall you are. What is the point of that? I seriously don't know, but it seems that all humans are required to take up far more space than they actually need. But don't get me wrong, as humans go you are not *that* disgusting.'

'Thanks . . . I think.'

'I mean, that Mary! Wow. I have never seen anything like her. She is so big and lumpy and hideous! And even though she has been drimwicked she can't do any magic at all. That's what I've heard.'

'Hey!' I said. 'Don't say that! Mary is one of the loveliest people in the whole world.'

The Truth Pixie looked sad, and stared down at a little purple flower beside her feet. 'Yes, she does seem very lovely, despite the way she looks.'

'Why does that make you sad?'

The Truth Pixie rolled her eyes and then put her hand over her mouth, as if desperately trying to stop the words coming out of her own mouth. 'Because she married the man of my dreams! Now, please, no more quest—'

'The man of your dreams?' I remembered her saying at the wedding, *I wish Father Christmas would stay on his own.* 'Father Christmas is the man of your dreams?'

'Aaagh!' wailed the Truth Pixie. 'Why? Why? Why do you ask questions like this? I am the Truth Pixie! I can do nothing but tell the truth and yet you keep asking the kind of questions that you really need to lie about. But I can't! I have to tell you the truth. I have to. It's my nature. I have to tell you that, yes, I am in love with Father Christmas and, yes, the day he married that lovely lumpy human woman was the saddest day of my life and, yes, every night I hug my pillow and pretend it is his big fat

93

soft belly and, yes, on Christmas Eve I stayed awake worrying in case something terrible happened to him.' The pixie panted, as if the truth was a long run that had exhausted her.

I just stood there, a little stunned. 'I'm sorry. I didn't realise. I just . . . I'm sorry.'

'I know. You are judging me. You are thinking it is wrong for a tiny little pixie like me to love a big ugly human like Father Christmas. But the truth is I am two hundred and eighty-four years old, which I know is quite young but it is not as young as him. And anyway, pixies often fall in love with other species. One of the Flying Story Pixies fell in love with a troll and she went to live with him. Well, inside his ear. But she died. She got trapped in there. Because of the ear wax. You see, that's the thing with trolls. They produce a lot of ear wax. Ah, poor old Flitter. But, yes, I must admit someone as, well, intelligent and charming as myself falling in love with a hairy ho–ho–ho–ing elf-loving *human* does seem a bit ridiculous, but what can you do? Love is love is love.'

I tried to take all this in. And then I remembered I was not here to talk about pixie love. I was here to get my cat. I had to get back to Elfhelm and show Kip his sleigh.

Then the Truth Pixie saw it – the broken sleigh – and Blitzen, as he made his way carefully through the trees.

'That's one of Father Christmas's reindeer, isn't it?'

'Yes.'

'What happened to the sleigh?'

I told the Truth Pixie what happened to the sleigh and she invited me inside, to sit down and have some cake and get my cat.

'I probably shouldn't. I'll get in trouble for being late.'

'I think you'll be in trouble anyway.'

'How much trouble do you think I'll be in? Tell me the truth.'

I knew she could do no other.

'A *lot* of trouble. The thing with elves is that although they act all jolly and fun and sing lots of Christmas songs, even if it is June, they are actually quite strict creatures. The reason they work so hard for Father Christmas in his workshop is because, on the inside, beneath their funny hats and jolly clothes, elves like order. They like discipline. They like following rules. They like everything to run smoothly. And when things go wrong – when someone makes a mistake – they tend to be very, very, very, very, very cross.'

'Oh no,' I said. 'Five verys. Just like Kip.'

'What?'

'Nothing. Listen, thank you very much for the offer of cake. It's really very kind of you. But I had better be going. Can I – erm – have my cat now, please?'

The Truth Pixie picked up Captain Soot and came back to hand him over. Captain Soot was quite heavy for the pixie to carry and her face was bright red from the effort.

'Are you *sure* it isn't a horse?'

'Yes. Absolutely.'

I leant forward to take Captain Soot from her. He was purring contentedly, clearly over the shock of what had happened earlier.

'There. There you go. You have him. From what you have told me, he sounds like he is cursed.'

'He's just a cat.'

'Well, goodbye. And please, please don't say anything to Father Christmas about, you know, me loving him or the pillow or anything like that.'

'I won't. I promise.'

'Promises are for liars. If you tell the truth all the time, you don't need promises.'

I smiled. 'Well, humans need promises. And I promise I won't say anything.'

And now Blitzen was right next to me, his snout near my shoulder as he looked down at the little pixie.

'This is Blitzen.'

The Truth Pixie scowled. 'I know who he is. He's Father Christmas's favourite reindeer. His special one. Maybe if I was big and smelly and had sticks coming out of my head he'd think I was special.'

'You *are* special,' I said. 'You're the Truth Pixie.'

She shook her head and looked down at her shoes. 'Yes. Exactly. I am the Truth Pixie. And who likes the truth? No one, that's who. You met the Lie Pixie, didn't you, on the worst day of my life?'

'The worst day of your life? Oh yes, the wedding.'

'Yes, well, he's my old boyfriend. He lives a little further south. Everyone likes him. He tells them exactly what they want to hear. He would tell you that humans are wonderful, and that having round ears is just as good as having pointed ears. He would tell you that when you got to Elfhelm you wouldn't be in any trouble at all and even if you were it would soon blow over and everything would be fine.'

'Yes,' I said, remembering how he had said he liked my ears. 'He's just being nice.'

'Yes. Exactly. But he isn't nice. You can't always know the truth about someone from what they say.'

I could see the sky through the criss-crossing branches of the forest. It was glowing a faint shade of pink. Sunset. It was about to get dark.

'I really had better go.'

'Yes, you really had.'

'How far away is Elfhelm now?' I asked.

'Just keep going straight down the hill until you see the tower of the Toy Workshop. Downhill walking is faster than uphill walking so you will probably be there in ten thousand minutes.'

'Ten thousand minutes? That's a long time.'

'That's pixie minutes. Pixie minutes are a lot shorter than other minutes. Ten thousand pixie minutes is actually quite short. It's the time it takes to bake a cake.'

'Right. Brilliant. Thank you, Truth Pixie.' And then, maybe because it was getting dark and more worries were starting to fill my brain, I asked the Truth Pixie something else. 'Do you know anything about the hole in the ground?'

'The hole?'

'Yes. There's a hole. Over there.' I pointed. 'That way.'

The Truth Pixie nodded. 'Oh yes, I have seen it.'

'Well, what do you think it is? Is it trolls? Rabbits? The Easter Bunny? Could it even be pixies?'

'I don't know.'

'I thought you were the Truth Pixie.'

'Yes. The *Truth* Pixie. Not the Knowledge Pixie. I don't know everything. I just tell the truth about the things I do know and have to admit when I don't know. But I do know that big holes in the middle of forests are generally *not good things*.'

'So what will Father Christmas say when I tell him?'

'Well, it will be a worry. And worries are the opposite of hope. And they steal it.'

'And if there's no hope,' I said, thinking aloud, 'there will be no Christmas. And Christmas is very nearly here.'

'Yes,' sighed the Truth Pixie, 'that is the truth.'

And so, as I left her, following the Truth Pixie's directions, and I began to see the colourful buildings of Elfhelm slowly emerge in the distance through the trees, I promised myself I would say nothing about the hole, or any of the other troubles I had found in the forest. The sleigh was going to be worry enough.

Cloudberry Pie

here was delicious steaming hot cloudberry pie. Father Christmas had baked it from Mary's recipe while she had been trying to put up the Christmas decorations with her mind, through the art of drimwickery, and failing miserably. Baubles were falling off the lop-sided Christmas tree, and paper snowflakes and chains were strewn all over the room.

We were all around the table, and in the middle of that table was the pie, ready to be eaten, but even that wasn't making things any better.

Father Christmas didn't tell me off. Not exactly. All he did when he heard the news was sigh and shake his head and look disappointed. In a way that was worse. Having Father Christmas look disappointed – and knowing you were the one person who had made him look disappointed – was a terrible feeling.

Mary sliced his pie and gave me a portion.

'Don't worry, dear,' she said. 'Worse things happen at sea. At least you're alive. That's the main thing, isn't it, Nikolas?'

'Yes,' he said. 'Absolutely.'

But he was still frowning. I wondered if there were any words I could say to make things better.

'Kip was very, very, very, very, very upset,' he said. 'He said he has never seen a sleigh in a worse state. The Barometer of Hope is irreparable. And his business is already struggling. He's worried he might have to close the school, and that people will be scared to fly his sleighs any more. Poor Kip.'

'Oh no,' I said.

'Oh yes.'

'It wasn't really my fault,' I said. 'I mean I didn't know that Captain Soot had followed me there. I didn't see him till the last minute. And then it was too late.'

'But you could have told Kip the cat was there, couldn't you?'

'But then Kip would have said I shouldn't go in the sleigh.'

'Well, in fairness, he would probably have been right.'

Guilt rose inside me, like a flood.

'I will help Kip to mend the sleigh,' I said.

Father Christmas shook his head. 'No.'

'No?'

'No. Kip is a very strange elf. I love him dearly but he is strange. He has peculiar ways. Unlike most elves he has never been very social. He doesn't like parties or anything like that. I once offered him a job in the Toy Workshop but he turned it down. He is the only elf – apart from Father Vodol, of course – who has ever turned me down. But really he is a very fragile elf. Because of what happened to him as a boy . . . Oh, Amelia, it is complicated. I know you didn't mean to do anything wrong but I also think we should try to make everything all right, don't you?'

I nodded. 'Yes. So what shall we do?'

Father Christmas scratched his beard. 'Well, the sleigh was very expensive. It was a Blizzard 360.'

'I know. Kip told me. A thousand chocolate coins.'

'Well, we'll pay it back.'

'How?' wondered Mary. 'They hardly pay us anything. *You* hardly pay us anything!'

'We'll have the money. Don't worry about that! In fact, let's go to the Bank of Chocolate right now and get the money!'

The Bank of Chocolate

I inhaled the smell of sweet sugary cocoa-y chocolate as Father Christmas pointed to the back of the bank where elf bank clerks were carrying huge bags of gold coins.

'You know what those coins are made of, don't you? Chocolate. All elf money is made of chocolate. The most delicious chocolate in the world.'

'I still find it so ridiculous!' Mary laughed.

And then Father Christmas went to a bank clerk, who was sitting behind a desk, with a name badge on that said 'SOVEREIGN'.

'Hello, Sovereign,' said Father Christmas.

'Hello, Father Christmas!' said Sovereign. She was smiling very excitedly. 'It's so lovely to see you! And these are the humans who live with you.'

'Yes, yes, this is Mary and Amelia.'

'Hello,' said Mary and I together.

Sovereign was giggling. 'Wow. Humans are so tall. They're nearly as tall as you, Father Christmas.'

'Well, technically I *am* a human. A drimwicked human but still a human. Now, Sovereign, I really need to get some money out of my bank account.'

'Of course, Father Christmas. How much money do you need?'

Father Christmas cleared his throat. 'Ummm, one thousand gold coins, please.'

Sovereign nearly fell off her chair. '*One thousand gold coins?*'

'Yes, please.'

Sovereign pulled out a book from under her desk. The book had writing on the front cover that said 'HOW MUCH MONEY EVERYONE HAS'.

'Oh,' said Sovereign. 'Oh. Oh.'

'Oh what?'

'Oh dear.'

'Oh dear what?'

'Oh dear, you haven't got enough money.'

'How much money do I have in my account?'

'You have eight hundred and thirty-seven coins. Which is strange, as you had twenty-three thousand, seven hundred and twenty-nine coins in your account last November.'

Father Christmas sighed, and looked a bit embarrassed. 'I . . . I . . . I ate most of them.'

Sovereign frowned and shook her head in disapproval. 'You shouldn't eat your money, Father Christmas.'

'But it is so delicious. And it was November. And I was getting stressed, with Christmas coming up. Why do you have to make it *so* delicious? This new chocolate you make it with is incredible.'

'Yes. It is Coco's new formula. We introduced it last autumn.'

'It makes no sense. If you don't want people to eat money, you shouldn't make it so tasty.'

Sovereign sighed. 'This is Elfhelm. Nothing

makes sense. For instance, it doesn't make sense that you are the Leader of the Elf Council *and* are in charge of the whole Toy Workshop and you only pay yourself fifty coins a month.'

'Well,' said Father Christmas, 'why should I pay myself more than the people who work for me? They work just as hard. And, besides, I don't do this for money.'

'Well, maybe you should,' said Sovereign.

Then Father Christmas turned to Sovereign and said, 'Could I have a loan? I only need another hundred and sixty-three gold coins.'

And then Sovereign scratched her head and thought and then she scratched her head some more. 'Yes. Yes, you can.'

'Brilliant.'

'But you will have to wait six months.'

'Six *months*?'

'Yes. Elves are good workers but very bad at paperwork. You know that. They're worse than pixies.'

Father Christmas frowned. 'Worse than pixies? No one's worse than pixies.'

'I'm sorry,' said Sovereign.

'No problem,' Father Christmas said. 'I will just save the money. We'll have it soon enough.'

'I'll go and earn the money somehow,' I said once we got back home.

Mary was shaking her head so hard I thought it might fall off. 'Don't be silly, Amelia. You go to school. You are eleven years old. You are far too young to have a job.'

I shrugged. 'I was cleaning the dirtiest, sootiest chimneys in London from the age of eight. I can work. I am made for working . . . I will go and ask Kip if he wants a hand at the School of Sleighcraft.'

Father Christmas sighed. 'I told you. He's a bit strange. He likes to work alone.'

'I know. But what if I went and just cleaned up for him when he wasn't there?'

'I think it's best if you stay away from Kip for a little while.'

Captain Soot jumped on my lap and began to purr, sensing something was wrong. I took a bite of pie I had saved from earlier. It was truly delicious. But I couldn't enjoy it. That was the thing about feeling guilty. It stole everything. Even the joy of a cloudberry pie.

'Well, I'll just have to start sweeping chimneys again.'

Mary's eyes grew wide in horror. 'Sweeping chimneys? Amelia! That was your old life.

That was the life you've been rescued from.'

'I know. But it's what I am good at. I'm not good at elf things. Sweeping chimneys is something I know. And, besides, it wasn't *that* bad. It wasn't as bad as the workhouse.'

Father Christmas was shaking his head. 'No, Amelia. You can't.'

'Why?'

'Have you *seen* the size of elf chimneys? You'd never fit inside one.'

He had a point. Elf chimneys – like elf everything else – were a lot smaller than human ones.

'There is literally no way you'd be able to climb up an elf chimney. And if you did, you would never come out.'

'But you fit in all kinds of chimneys.'

'Not elf ones, as a rule. And, anyway, that's different. I've been drimwicked. I'm magic.'

'Why can't I be drimwicked?' I asked. It felt horrible being the least magical creature in the whole of Elfhelm. I was even less magical than Captain Soot because he was a cat and cats were magical simply because they were cats.

'You know why, Amelia. You can only be drimwicked if you are dead – or nearly dead. It is the drimwick that brings back life. You can't just drimwick someone. Drimwicks are about true and real hope. You can't fake them. And they are very risky.'

'And being drimwicked doesn't mean you can do drimwickery,' said Mary. 'I was drimwicked nearly a year ago. And I've been taking those classes every week and I still can't float in the air or move things with my mind or stop time or any of that. I mean, look at these decorations.'

We all looked around the room and started to giggle.

'I can't even spickle dance.' Mary chuckled.

Father Christmas touched Mary's hand. 'It will happen, sweetbread. In time.'

Mary sighed as she stared at me. 'Anyway, you are magic enough just as you are, Amelia.'

It was my turn to sigh now. It was a long one.

Then Father Christmas's eyes sparkled a little. 'I know!' he said. 'You can work in the Toy Workshop.'

'The Toy Workshop?'

'Yes. On Saturday. And not just any Saturday. It's the Saturday before Christmas. In the week before Christmas elves get paid two hundred chocolate coins a day.'

'But what if I'm not very good?'

Father Christmas laughed as if I was being ridiculous. 'Of course you'll be good.'

'But at school I am rubbish at toymaking.'

Father Christmas flapped his hand in the air as if my worry was a fly that could be batted away. 'The thing about the Toy Workshop is that it isn't just about *making* toys. There is plenty to do there. We'll find you something.'

I smiled. I was worried, but I didn't want to be more of a nuisance than I had already proven to be. 'All right, then,' I said. 'What time will I start?'

'Very Early Indeed. Which is the elf's favourite hour.'

I nearly said, 'But I'm not an elf!' But didn't. I just said it in my head instead.

The Greatest Magic of All

o it was that I came to be in the vast gingerbread-walled hall of the Toy Workshop at Very Early Indeed on the Saturday before Christmas.

I had never been there before and it was an amazing sight, seeing all the elves – hundreds of them – hard at work.

Father Christmas showed me round the place, pointing out different things.

We passed a large circular table of elves who were stitching teddy bears and cuddly reindeer and puppy toys at high speed. It was scary watching the needles stitch so quickly. Father Christmas saw me go a little pale.

'Don't worry,' he said. 'You won't be sewing cuddly toys. The elves who work on cuddly toys are the most experienced toymakers in Elfhelm. In the run-up to Christmas they can make a thousand teddy bears an hour, each.'

We walked on.

We passed another table with a giant red printing machine where an elf was pressing big green buttons. As he pushed the controls different books would fly out of the top of the huge machine and land into different elf hands.

'Books,' said Father Christmas, 'are the greatest gifts of all. Nothing else comes close.'

I saw *Oliver Twist* by Charles Dickens – my favourite author, and a man I'd once met – shoot out of the machine. An elf wearing glasses caught the book, opened it up and began to read.

'I could do that,' I said, watching the elf read the book and check for mistakes. 'That would be my perfect job and it looks . . .'

I was about to say 'easy' but I soon saw that it wasn't easy at all. The elf was reading it faster than I had seen anyone read a book. Her fingers were turning a page every second, and her head nodded up and down so fast as she read each page her hat nearly fell off.

'That is Annabel. She is the fastest reader we have.'

As we made our way through the room it suddenly became warmer. I looked around and saw lots of trees with thousands of tiny oranges hanging from them.

DO NOT
DISTURB

'These are the satsuma trees,' Father Christmas explained. 'You see, I thought it would be a nice touch to leave a satsuma in a lot of the stockings. Something different. Satsumas! Father Topo thought I was crazy, but I knew the children would like it. They'd always remember that magic wasn't just about toys. It can be everywhere. It can be a fruit growing on a tree. We plan it so they are perfectly ripe on Christmas Eve.'

Then the room became cooler again and we approached a noisy section of the workshop. Hundreds of balls were being tested by getting thrown or bounced or juggled.

Nearby there was a table full of elves hunched over metal spinning tops, shaping them with hammers, or painting them, or spinning them.

'This is the section where I thought we would start you off,' said Father Christmas happily. 'It's the part of the workshop where most new elves start.'

Again, the unspoken words came to me: *But I am not an elf.* Still, I kept smiling and said, 'Right. So, err, what do I do?'

'That is a question for Humdrum. Come on, Amelia. Let's go and meet him.'

'Here he is,' said Father Christmas as he patted on the back a nervous-looking elf in a blue-and-white striped outfit that was slightly too small for him. The elf nearly lost his balance and in the process his glasses fell off. 'Humdrum is the Assistant Deputy Chief Maker of Toys That Spin or Bounce,' explained Father Christmas.

Humdrum blushed and pushed his glasses back on.

'Humdrum is one of our hardest workers. And even though he is only an assistant deputy, on weekends he is actually the main elf in charge of *all* the spinning and bouncing toys. Hello, Humdrum!'

'H-h-h-hello, Father Christmas,' said Humdrum, who was bouncing a ball and marking the height of the bounce with the help of an elf with a tape measure beside him.

'You know Amelia, don't you? She is a human.'

Humdrum nodded, and quietly whispered, 'That's right, that's right.'

'She'd like to start working in the workshop. Just on weekends. Because even though she is taller than every elf in this room she is actually only eleven years old and has to go to school.'

'Hello, Humdrum,' I said and held out my hand.

Humdrum seemed quite terrified by my hand. Maybe it was the size of it. But he shook it politely.

'Hello, A-Amelia,' he said.

'Right,' said Father Christmas, 'I'll leave you with Humdrum. He'll show you what to do. And I'll see you in ten hours.'

'*Ten hours?*' I spluttered, but Father Christmas was already walking away. I turned back to Humdrum. 'What would you like me to do?'

'Spinning tops,' he said. 'Follow me.'

Toys That Spin or Bounce

I started work on the spinning-top table. I was first given the job of hammering the spinning tops into shape, because Humdrum thought I would be strong, being a human. And I was strong. Stronger than I looked. All those years of climbing chimneys meant my arms were as strong as most grown-up humans. Maybe I was a bit *too* strong, because I kept putting dents in the metal. So then I was given the job of painting the spinning tops, but that was even harder. If you ever get a spinning top for Christmas, you will see that they normally have very intricate patterns on them that look like they took days to paint. But the truth is an elf can paint an entire spinning top in a few seconds.

The best elf painter in the workshop was (and probably still is) a woman elf called Spiral, who had her hair styled into five tight little buns and who had red spirals painted onto her cheeks. I sat next to her, as Humdrum had instructed. And then Spiral told me what to do.

'First, take a paintbrush from the pot.'

I took a paintbrush from the pot.

'Then, put the green paint on the paintbrush.'

I put the green paint on the paintbrush.

'Now, spin the spinning top in front of you.'

I spun the spinning top in front of me.

'Right. Very good, Amelia. Now, paint the spinning top.'

I turned to Spiral. 'So you want me to paint it *while it is spinning*?'

'Of course! How else would you paint it.'

I shrugged. 'Maybe not spinning?'

Spiral shook her head. 'Don't be silly. That would take for ever.' She handed me a piece of card with a pretty but very complicated pattern on it. 'This is the pattern chart. We have to do three thousand of these today.'

'*Three thousand?* How many elves are working on them.'

'Just me, Lupin over there, and you. A thousand each.' She noticed the spinning top in front of me was beginning to wobble. 'Quick! Get spinning! Get painting. Then I can press the button.'

'What button?'

She pointed to the top button on her outfit. A perfectly ordinary round green button. 'As soon as I press this button the spinning tops speed out of that chute, one by one. You spin, you paint, then on with the next one. Now, off you go. The paint pots are all in front of you.'

So I began. I spun the spinning top and tried to follow the pattern. I pressed the paintbrush against the metal and the spinning top immediately fell over and onto the floor with a loud clank. And before I knew it another spinning top was in front of me.

'Don't worry,' said Spiral. 'Try the next one. A bit lighter with the brush this time.'

And this time at least I managed not to make the spinning top fall over. Not straight away, at least. I pressed the brush, covered in green paint, very daintily onto the moving top and tried to follow the zigzag pattern on the card.

'Oh dear,' said Spiral, as Lupin couldn't help giggling at my effort. 'You will have to be faster than that! The whole thing needs to be painted and perfect by the time the top stops spinning.'

So I tried to go faster, but by the time it stopped spinning Lupin's laughter was even louder. The spinning top was just a big mess of green and red paint. It was the worst-looking spinning top I had ever seen.

And not only that: I had taken so long there were now three spinning tops in front of me waiting to be painted – now four, no, wait, five!

'Keep going,' said Spiral. 'You'll get the hang of it.'

But of course I didn't get the hang of it. I kept on spinning the tops and painting and spinning and painting and spinning and painting until I felt dizzy. And as I tried to go faster I was less careful with the paint, and, just as

Humdrum came over to check on how I was getting along, I got a big drippy blob of green paint on the end of the brush and when it touched one of the tops the paint went flying and splattered over Spiral and Lupin and Humdrum and me.

Humdrum was the one who was most covered because he had been leaning in to have a closer look.

'Don't worry,' he said, wiping the mess from his glasses. 'It's only a bit of paint.'

There was another clank – and another – as unpainted spinning tops kept on crashing onto the floor.

The latest spinning top I had been painting fell too, and Spiral picked it up for Humdrum to inspect.

Humdrum gulped as he stared at the swirling mess of paint. 'Maybe,' he said, 'this could go in the stocking of a very naughty child.'

'I don't know if anyone has been *that* naughty,' added Spiral unhelpfully.

'I'm sorry,' I said, feeling too human. 'I was trying my hardest.'

Humdrum, splattered with green paint, smiled meekly. 'D-d-don't worry. It's just a little crazy in here. With C-C-Christmas so close.

Maybe you should do some bounce testing instead.'

So I did some bounce testing.

Bounce testing sounded simple. You were meant to bounce a ball on the ground as hard as you could and then see how high it reached. However you also had to measure the bounce with a tape measure. So, bouncing the ball was easy enough but then you had to measure how high the ball reached. But that was impossible, because I couldn't be fast enough with the tape measure.

And then Father Christmas appeared and asked Humdrum, 'How is everything going?' just as one of my balls bounced on his head. 'And why have you got green paint all over your face?'

'Err . . . well . . . the thing is . . .' said Humdrum.

So I decided to help him out. I wanted to tell the truth. 'The thing is, it was me. It was my fault. It turned out that . . .'

Father Christmas caught sight of the spinning tops – the messy ones I had been painting and the ones all over the floor.

'Oh dear,' he said.

Humdrum was still working on his answer

to Father Christmas. 'I d-d-don't know if the workshop is the best p-p-place for a human.'

'I'm sure we can find something you are good at,' said Father Christmas warmly, a kind gleam in his eyes.

'But there is nothing I am good at apart from cleaning chimneys.'

Father Christmas looked quite cross. 'Nothing you are good at! Don't be so silly. This isn't the Amelia I know. The Amelia who survived the scariest workhouse in London. There is plenty you are good at.'

'Like?'

'Like bravery. You are the bravest girl I know. And Christmas-saving. You are very good at Christmas-saving.'

'Those aren't *jobs*,' I said, with a bit of a scowl on my face.

I could see he was struggling to think of the things I was good at. But then his eyes lit up and he clapped his hands as he thought of something.

'*Writing!*' he exclaimed.

'What?'

'I bumped into Mother Jingle today. She told me she had read your story about the cat who got stuck up a chimney, and she said she had never read anything like it. She thought it was amazing.'

'Really? She said that?'

'She certainly did. And you enjoy writing too, don't you?'

I nodded. 'It's my favourite thing. After reading. But really reading and writing are the same thing. Writing is just reading a story that is in your mind and putting it on paper.'

'Well, you are very good at it. You could be the next Mr Dickens. Maybe you should write a book.'

'That would probably take too long,' I said. 'I write at human speed. Not elf speed.'

But now Humdrum was doing something I hadn't seen him do all day. He was smiling. 'I know,' he said sheepishly. 'I mean, I m-m-might know. Possibly. Maybe. Perhaps.'

'What do you know?' asked Father Christmas.

He took his glasses off, then put them on again. He bit his top lip. 'Well – and this is just an idea – but I-I-I was just thinking that maybe Amelia could work for Noosh.'

'Noosh?' I said.

'My wife. She's called N-N-Noosh. She was, um, named after her mother's favourite sneeze.'

'Yes, I know who she is.'

'She's the editor of the *Daily Snow*. She took over from Father Vodol. I am very proud of her. She is the cleverest elf in all of Elfhelm. She knows some of the longest words in the world. Like . . . like . . . antidrimwickification and squasipetulabumpkinbreath.' He took his glasses off again and tried to wipe away the remaining bits of green paint. 'She is looking for new writers. You see, Father Vodol has set up a new newspaper to try to beat the *Daily Snow*.'

'No,' said Father Christmas, looking worried but trying his best to smile through it. 'I have heard the rumours too, but he assured me he was doing nothing of the sort.'

Humdrum sighed. 'Well, there is a new newspaper being sold right now on the Main

Path, as of today. It's called the D-D-D-*Daily Truth*. Noosh is convinced it's the work of Father Vodol.'

And I remembered what Father Vodol had said to me on the day of the wedding: *Oh, you don't understand the mind of elves. You see, they are very changeable. You take one wrong step and they'll turn against you. You'll see. I'll make sure of it.*

I thought of all my wrong steps. Like crashing the sleigh.

'Well, I doubt he'd start a paper called the *Daily Truth*.' Father Christmas laughed. 'The last thing Father Vodol is interested in is the truth.' But then he scratched his beard, confused. 'How can a newspaper just appear? Where are its offices?' He tried to shake away the thought. 'Anyway, the trouble is, Humdrum, that Amelia goes to school five days a week.'

'I could work on weekends, just like here,' I said, and suddenly the thought shone inside me like a sun. Suddenly I felt at home again. 'That would be amazing! I could be a real-life journalist!'

Father Christmas laughed a little. 'Okay, Amelia. Why not? Let's find Noosh.'

The Daily Snow

I sat on the top floor of the *Daily Snow* office building in a chair made of gingerbread with giant bright red fluffy cushions. Almost everything in the room – apart from the cushions – was made of gingerbread. Even the walls. Although it wasn't ordinary gingerbread. No. This was *reinforced* extra-strong gingerbread, and it shone a deep dark brownish orange. The office had only a single window, a giant round one at the end of the room, complete with a view of all the curving streets and small multicoloured houses of Elfhelm. On the walls were lots of old front pages of the *Daily Snow* hanging in large golden picture frames.

Noosh herself sat behind a huge desk and stared at me for a long time with wide open eyes from beneath her wild black hair.

She looked tired. Even the bags under her eyes had bags. But, despite that, she was quite animated, and moved her hands around a lot, and smiled, even as she frowned.

'I have to get up Very Early Indeed every morning. Sometimes even earlier. I have to wake up, have breakfast, make a snow elf with Little Mim – he insists I make one every morning – before taking him to kindergarten. Well, sometimes Humdrum takes him. It depends on his shift, really.' She picked up the cup in front of her and took a sip. 'Triple-strength hot chocolate with extra chocolate sprinkles. It's the only thing that gets me through the day. You're sure you don't want one?'

'Yes,' I told her. 'I'm sure. Thank you, though. Too much chocolate gives me a headache.'

'Wow. Must be hard to fit in to Elfhelm then?'

'A little,' I said, when really I meant, *Yes! A lot! I feel like a freak!*

'So. You are good at writing, I hear?'

'Well, I know that I enjoy it.'

'The thing is that writing for a newspaper is very different to writing stories that you make up from your head.'

'Yes,' I said, 'I understand.'

She saw me looking at one of the old *Daily Snow* front pages. The headline was 'CHRISTMAS FOR HUMANS – A VERY BAD IDEA!'

'Ah,' Noosh explained, 'that was back in the old days. Back when Father Vodol was in charge. He believed the way to sell a newspaper was to make elves hate humans. To try and keep elves thinking just of themselves and fearing strangers. He once started a campaign to try to build a wall stretching from sea to sea, and rising right over the mountain, in order to keep humans out.'

I spotted another framed front page headline: 'BUILD THAT WALL!' And another: 'NEW RESEARCH: HUMANS ARE POINT-LESSLY TALL!' And another, so long it hardly fitted on the page: 'HUMANS ONCE KIDNAPPED LITTLE KIP AND SO THEY ARE ALL PROBABLY KIDNAPPERS (DON'T TRUST THEM, WHATEVER FATHER CHRISTMAS TELLS YOU!' And: 'ELVES FOR ELVES: VOTE VODOL!' And: 'TROLL TERROR STOPS CHRISTMAS!'

Noosh pointed at the pile of newspapers on her desk. 'This is today's paper,' she explained. 'Look at the headline.'

I looked. It said 'HOW TO MAKE A CANDLE OUT OF EARWAX'.

She opened a drawer and pulled out another newspaper. 'This is yesterday's paper. Look again at the headline. "SLEIGH BELLES' SINGER SAYS HER SORE THROAT IS A BIT BETTER NOW"'.

'We devoted ten pages to that. Had a full interview with Juniper and everything.'

I smiled. 'I like the Sleigh Belles.'

Noosh nodded. 'Of course you do. Everyone likes the Sleigh Belles. "Reindeer Over The Mountain" is the greatest song ever written, in my opinion. And everyone loves "It's Very Nearly Christmas (I Am So Excited I Have Wet My Tunic)". You've heard that one, right?'

'I'm not sure.'

'Well, it's great. But the trouble is Juniper's sore throat shouldn't be on the front page of a newspaper. It's important, yes, obviously. But is it *that* important? I don't think so.'

I leant back in my chair, inhaling the scent of gingerbread, and asked the obvious question: 'Why did you put it on the front page, then?'

Noosh nodded as if I had said something very clever. Then she stood up and kept on nodding. She beckoned me over to the large round window at the far end of the room. The one with the panoramic view of Elfhelm.

'Come over here,' she said. 'I want to show you something.'

I went over and had a look. The *Daily Snow* office building was – after the tower of the Toy Workshop – the tallest building in the whole of Elfhelm. It was located in the centre of Elfhelm, at the end of Vodol Street.

From here, on the top floor, I could see Blitzen and the other reindeer over in Reindeer Field. I saw the village hall. I saw an elf walk into the clog shop on the Main Path. I saw another carrying a little bag of chocolate coins he'd just withdrawn from the Bank of Chocolate. I could see the Street of Seven Curves and all the little elf cottages sitting silently. I could see Quiet Street and Really Quiet Street looking quiet and really quiet, respectively. I could see the Toy Workshop and the School of Sleighcraft and the University of Advanced Toymaking.

Beyond that, to the west, I could see the Wooded Hills. And to the south the vast snow-covered crooked triangle that was Very Big Mountain. Beyond *that*, of course, out of view, was the rest of Lapland, and Finland. The world of humans. The world of tall round-eared people who looked like me.

'What do you see?' Noosh whispered, as if the question had come from the air itself.

'A lot,' I said. 'Everything. The whole of Elfhelm.'

Noosh nodded again. 'Yes. You see everything. Of course, it is everything. But do you know what you also see?'

'No. What?'

'*Nothing.*'

I was confused, and probably looked it too. 'What do you mean?'

'I mean this *everything* is also *nothing*. Nothing actually *happens* here. I mean, yes, sure, things *happen*. Elves go to school or the workshop. Members of the Elf Council go to their meetings at the village hall to discuss sleigh flight restrictions and reindeer permits. People

137

buy clogs and weave tunics. They sing and spickle dance and say kind things to each other. They work hard and play hard, but the problem is nothing really *happens*. Nothing has happened since the troll stuff? And you saw the front page when we welcomed you – a human girl into Elfhelm. Look, we put that up on the wall too.'

I had seen it. 'THE GIRL WHO SAVED CHRISTMAS' ran the headline. And there was a colour picture of me too.

'Do you like the picture?'

'Yes, I suppose it's okay.'

'Mother Miro painted it. She's the *Daily Snow*'s in-house picture painter. She's very good. And it was a very good news item. Indeed, you have been one of the more interesting things to happen this year. The incident with the sleigh, for instance . . .'

'Oh no. Did you write about that?'

Noosh shook her head. 'Not yet. I wanted to speak to you first, actually, and maybe do an interview about it.'

'Maybe I could write it?' I suggested hopefully. 'That was what I was thinking, you see, that maybe you'd let me write about what it is like to be a human in an elf world.'

But Noosh was already shaking her head. 'A human in an elf world? No, no, no. That wouldn't work. You see, the sleigh crash story is interesting because people would wonder if you died or not, but if you wrote the story they would know you didn't die and that would be disappointing – in a journalistic sense.'

'Well, what about the weather? It's very windy today. I could write about the windiness.'

'Wind is not news unless it breaks or hurts something.'

'Or Christmas. It's very nearly Christmas. I could write about human Christmas traditions.'

She was shaking her head. 'The elves invented most of them.'

I felt a bit hopeless, then. A little lost. The way things were going I was beginning to think there was no way Noosh was going to offer me work.

'The trouble is,' she said, as we stared out of the window, 'that apart from the sleigh crash and Juniper's sore throat and Father Casper the Candlemaker's discovery that you can make candles out of ear wax *there is no news*. Not really. Not since we made peace with the trolls again. No one dies. There is no war. Christmas isn't under threat. It makes Elfhelm very lovely to live in, but it also means no one wants to buy newspapers.'

Just then I noticed something on the Main Path.

A long queue of elves by the newspaper stand.

'But look,' I said. 'Those elves seem very keen to buy a newspaper.'

Noosh made a groaning sound and grabbed her head as if she wanted to pull her own hair out. 'Yes, yes, they do! The trouble is the newspaper they are buying isn't the *Daily Snow*.'

'It isn't?'

'Nope. It's the new paper. Have you seen it yet? Father Vodol's. The first edition. You see, when the Elf Council voted that he had to leave his job at the *Daily Snow* they didn't say that he couldn't start another newspaper. They assumed they didn't have to. By making him live on Very Quiet Street and by taking away his newspaper offices they thought he wouldn't – especially after the Elf Council took all his money. But he has probably got a lot of chocolate coins hidden away somewhere. Years ago, when he was Leader of the Elf Council, he paid himself ten thousand chocolate coins *a week*. And that's not to mention all the money he made from the *Daily Snow*. He hardly paid anyone here anything at all. When I was Chief Reindeer Correspondent I was lucky if I got thirty chocolate coins for a whole week.'

'Oh dear,' I said, now seeing the flag above the stand, waving in the breeze: THE DAILY TRUTH.

Noosh laughed the kind of laugh that didn't really sound like a laugh at all. 'The *Daily Truth*! Of course, it's not really the truth. Father Vodol doesn't care about the truth. He doesn't care about anything except selling papers. And the way he sells papers is by lying. By making everyone scared of things that don't exist. When he set up the *Daily Snow* years ago he made up things about pixies and trolls and rabbits and humans. He tried to get elves to be scared. Oh, but you know what he is saying, don't you? What he's been saying since I took over his job here?'

'What is he saying?'

'He was saying – *is* saying – that *I* am the one making things up. He calls us fake. But I have never *once* published a story that isn't true. What would the point of that be? A newspaper that didn't report the news?'

'Not much point, I'd imagine.'

Noosh sighed a long and exasperated sigh. 'It's a mystery.'

'Why?'

'Where is it? Where is the *Daily Truth*'s office? Where is he printing the newspaper? It isn't easy running a newspaper. You can't just make it appear . . .' She leaned her head against the glass and closed her eyes. 'No, it really isn't easy.'

We left the window and sat back down again.

'I'm sorry,' she said, 'but we are losing money. I'm afraid that without any exciting news stories – news stories that you could prove to be completely *true* – I simply can't afford to take new people on.'

I tried one last time to think of an exciting news story, but my mind was as blank as a field in the snow.

I could see that she was upset about the whole situation and I didn't want to make her feel worse, so I just said, 'Oh, never mind. I'll be going then.'

And I stood up.

But just as I did so something slapped against the window. It was a newspaper. A copy of the *Daily Truth* that must have blown out of someone's hands and floated its way in the wind up to the window. The front page pressed against the glass, facing us.

'Oh no,' said Noosh. 'Look away. Don't read that nonsense.'

But it was too late. I'd already seen the picture beneath the headline. It was of me. But, unlike the other picture, whoever painted this one was trying to make me look as angry as possible. Beside it, smaller, was a picture of the Blizzard 360 looking even more smashed up than it did in real life.

I saw the headline and read it out: 'ENEMY AMONG US.'

I even had time to read the first two lines: 'The adopted human of Father Christmas, Amelia Wishart, should not be trusted. She seeks to destroy as much as Elfhelm as possible, starting with this sleigh . . .'

'Oh no,' said Noosh. 'Listen, Amelia . . .'

I tried to read on but the paper blew away, flapping in the wind like a desperate bird.

'I'm not an enemy,' I said. 'I don't want to destroy Elfhelm. It was an accident. I couldn't help it.'

'I know that, Amelia. Every elf with goodness in their hearts knows that.'

'But you've just said that more people will read the *Daily Truth* than the *Daily Snow*. Hundreds of elves are going to read this . . .' I began thinking aloud. 'I'll show them. I'll make things right. I'll pay back the sleigh . . . Then you can write about it.'

Noosh frowned, deep in thought. 'I wish I could give you the money. But, unless you find a big story that involves *something happening* and that can be *proven to be true*, I can't use it. If we can sell newspapers with the truth, then I can pay you.'

'What about the story of my innocence? What if we write about what really happened?

About how Captain Soot jumped into the sleigh and then onto Blitzen and that made Blitzen go crazy and then Captain Soot fell out of my arms and we dived to save him and I had to cut the sleigh free. Why don't we write about that?'

'Well, I'd love to. But can you prove it? Do you have any witnesses?'

'I'm afraid not.'

'It would probably just lead to Father Vodol making up more stories. And the trouble is his stories will be bigger because they'll be lies, and the thing about lies is that they don't have a height limit. They can be as big and tall as he wants them to be.'

'So it's no use then,' I said. 'The truth can never beat lies.'

Noosh was shaking her head. 'Don't believe that. We can't believe that. We've just got to find a truth as big as any lie Father Vodol could come up with. An *impossible* truth.' She whispered that swear word. 'The story to end all stories. That is my dream. To make the *Daily Snow* the most popular newspaper in Elfhelm once again. And then we can correct all of Father Vodol's lies.'

I tried to think where I could find a giant

news story but I still couldn't think of anything. The only thing going around my head was what Father Christmas was going to say when he read the first edition of Father Vodol's newspaper.

'I'm sorry,' I said to Noosh. 'I'd really better go.'

The Outsider

I walked home feeling the cold bite of the wind. I passed a couple of elves fresh from the workshop who smiled at me and said, 'Hello, Amelia!' And I said hello back and thought maybe it wasn't so bad. Maybe not *that* many people were going to read the *Daily Truth* today. But when I turned off Vodol Street onto Main Path a little elf girl pointed up at me, saying, 'Look, Mummy! That's the human girl!'

And then her mummy – a round rosy-cheeked elf I had never seen before – grabbed her child's arm and pulled her close. 'Stay away from her! She's dangerous! She doesn't belong here!'

The little girl elf stared at me, open-mouthed, and then burst into tears, her wails scratching at me like a cat's claws.

I hurried past them.

At the newspaper stand everyone in the queue was mumbling and whispering about me. The newspaper seller, a kind old elf with wispy grey hair, gave me a sympathetic look

and said, 'I'm sorry, love. I just sell the stuff. I don't write it.'

'It's all right,' I told him, and tried not to cry, even as I felt the sadness build and build and build inside me.

But then I felt my eyes hot with tears and I began to run.

'YES! RUN AWAY!' said a voice behind me. 'WE DON'T WANT YOUR KIND HERE!'

I ran past the Bank of Chocolate and Mother Mayhem's Music Shop and Clogs! Clogs! Clogs! and Red & Green, the clothes shop, and Magic Books, the bookshop, and then I found myself at Reindeer Field. Suddenly there were no elves, just reindeer, and reindeer didn't read newspapers, so I felt safer, but I kept running all the way, as Blitzen looked up to see what the matter was. On and on and on. Until I was home. And I knocked on the door and kept knocking and there was no answer, but then I remembered that I didn't need a key as it was Elfhelm and people left their doors open, so I turned the handle and went inside and I cried. I cried and cried and cried.

I went into the living room, full of decorations, and saw Captain Soot asleep in his basket beside the Christmas tree. I stared at the darkness of the fireplace. There was something comforting about the dark. I went over and crouched down, into the fireplace, and just stared at it. But then I heard footsteps on the path and saw Mary outside the window humming to herself and carrying a basket full of berries.

She must have been to the Wooded Hills, collecting fruit for the Christmas cake she was planning to make.

She hadn't seen me.

I didn't want her to see me.

I didn't want to see anyone. Or talk to anyone.

I didn't want to cry in front of Mary and make her sad. But in seconds she would open the door and be inside the house.

So I then did the thing I was best at in the whole world. I crawled up the chimney.

Unlike elf houses, Father Christmas's home had been made to a human scale, and that included the chimney. So it was easy for me to fit inside. Halfway up I pressed my feet and back against the opposite sides of the sooty chimney wall and waited there, with my knees quite close to my chest, and cried some more.

I wanted to stay there for ever.

Unseen, in the darkness, not bothering or offending anyone.

As I cried it dawned on me – I wasn't made for anywhere. I would never fit in, no matter where I was. In London, at the workhouse, I was the one that Mr Jeremiah Creeper hated the most. I had never fitted in. Even before that, being a *girl* chimney sweep had made me a kind of freak among other children. And now, here, it was happening again. Here of all places,

where I thought life would be wonderful and magical. Where I thought I would be happy for ever.

But I wasn't crying for me.

Well, not *just* for me.

I was crying because I had now made things harder for Father Christmas. The whole of Elfhelm was probably going to turn on him now.

As I tried hard to stop sobbing, I heard something below.

A voice.

'Amelia?'

I looked down and in the darkness saw Mary's face staring up at me. She was leaning into the fireplace and looked understandably surprised to see me there.

'What are you doing up there, sweetheart?'

'I just wanted to be on my own.'

'Well, we all want to be on our own sometimes. I certainly do. But I tend to just go to my room and shut the door. I don't climb up a chimney.'

'I like chimneys,' I told her. 'I know what to do in a chimney. Unlike everywhere else.'

'Come and have some berries and tell me what's the matter.'

I did as she said. I came down.

'Look at your face,' she said. 'All that soot. All those tears.'

I looked in the mirror. The tears had made little tracks through the soot.

'What's happened, Amelia? What's wrong?'

I thought of the front page of the *Daily Truth*. I thought of the sleigh. I thought of school. I thought of the workshop. I thought of nearly being eaten by a tree. I thought of Father Vodol, who had been against me from the start. I thought of the faces staring at me on the Main Path, near the newspaper stand. 'Everything.'

And I told her. I told her it all. Then – when Father Christmas came home – Mary told him too.

But Father Christmas knew.

'I saw the newspaper,' he said, as he sat on his rocking chair with Captain Soot purring on his lap. 'Father Vodol is up to his old tricks again.'

'I'm so sorry,' I said. 'I should never have stayed here. I should go back to London. You should fly me there tonight.'

'Don't be silly, Amelia,' said Mary.

'But I don't belong here.'

'Nonsense! Of course you belong here.'

But just as he said that a short elf with a green-and-white hat walked by the window and saw me and shouted in, 'You don't belong here!'

Father Christmas stormed to the door, flung it open, and roared, 'Get away from here with your stinking words, Dewdrop. It's Father Vodol's poisonous lies that don't belong here!'

'I'm sorry, Father Christmas,' said Dewdrop. 'But the human girl is here to destroy Elfhelm and all we stand for. It was in the *Daily Truth*. And it wouldn't be called the *Daily Truth* if it wasn't the truth, would it?'

I could see through the doorway there were other elves gathering. This day really was the worst.

The Elves on the Doorstep

One thing about elves that I had noticed is that they like being in a crowd. Elf crowds gathered very easily. If there were two elves standing still on a street, within a minute it would be thirty elves, and in ten minutes it would be three hundred. The crowd was getting bigger by the second.

'The real story,' said Father Topo, who was now on the doorstep, 'is that Father Vodol is clearly trying to poison our minds again. We should have been tougher with him.'

Father Christmas sighed. 'We took away his offices and made him live on Very Quiet Street.'

'That wasn't enough. He has always been trouble. We should have locked him up, Father Christmas, when we found out he'd set the trolls against us.'

'Now, now, Father Topo. We shouldn't lock *anyone* up. That isn't the Elfhelm way. That hasn't been the Elfhelm way since ... since ... well, since Father Vodol locked *me* up when I was a little boy. And Father Vodol isn't in charge any more.'

'He might as well be,' said Father Topo sadly. Even his white moustache seemed to wilt with sadness. 'Almost everyone is reading the *Daily Truth* right now. It's only been going for a few hours and it's already the most popular paper. And it doesn't help that the *Daily Snow*'s circulation is down to only seventeen readers. Poor Noosh.'

'The *Daily Snow* is *boring*!' said an elf at the back of the crowd.

'It never tells the truth!' said another.

'That's right,' said Dewdrop. 'It never tells the truth. That's why it's so boring.'

'It *always* tells the truth, now Noosh is in charge,' corrected Father Topo.

Father Christmas, from the doorway, looked around at the growing mass of elves. 'Now, now, everyone, let's all calm down. We mustn't believe Father Vodol's lies about humans. He's been telling them for years. Humanophobia has no place in Elfhelm.'

'What's humanophobia?' asked Little Mim, who was – I could now see – holding on to her great-great-great-great-great-great-grandfather Father Topo's hand.

'Humanophobia is an irrational fear of humans,' explained Father Topo, rather quietly, but still loud enough for some of the elves to hear. One of them stepped forwards. Thin and tall with a bit of a stoop, I recognised him instantly. My heart began to beat like a drum. It was Kip.

'Maybe it's not an irrational fear,' he said.

The elves all turned to stare at him. Kip was

an elf whom other elves were a little intimidated by. And although he spoke to elf children when he was teaching them to fly sleighs, he rarely spoke to elf grown-ups.

'In fact, there is every reason to be scared of humans.'

Several elves muttered and nodded in agreement.

Father Christmas had a pained expression, as if he had just trodden on something sharp. 'But, Kip,' he said. 'Look at me. I am a human.'

'And so was your father,' said Kip. Some of the crowd gasped. 'Everyone knows the story about your father kidnapping *me*.'

I gulped. So that was why Kip had gone white as snow when he met me.

I went over to stand beside Father Christmas, to try to give him some support. As I looked up I saw his eyes bulge and glisten with tears that didn't quite fall, before he managed to blink them away. 'Kip, you know how sorry I am about what happened to you. My father was a complicated man.'

Kip shook his head. 'A complicated *kidnapper*.'

Father Christmas turned around to check that Mary couldn't hear. But she was busy heating up the berries in the kitchen, singing loudly to herself. He turned back to the crowd – to Kip – and spoke softly.

'Listen, Kip, I am not my father. There are good humans and there are bad humans, and sometimes there are humans with bits of good and bits of bad.' He was speaking louder now, for everyone to hear. 'Humans aren't really different to elves, you know. It's just that when lives are deprived of magic, things can be quite miserable. And miserable lives can make people do miserable things. That's why we decided to help them, wasn't it? That's why we decided to give the humans some magic in their lives, even if it was for one day? That's right, isn't it?'

'That's right!' said Father Topo.

'That's right!' said Father Bottom.

'That's right!' said Little Mim.

'That's right!' said Mother Breer, who was carrying a shiny new black belt over her arm for Father Christmas.

'That's right!' said Mother Miro, who had already set up her easel and canvas, and was beginning to paint the whole scene.

'That's r-i-i-i-i-g-h-t!' sang Juniper and the other Sleigh Belles.

And a few other elves whose names I didn't

know also said, 'That's right', and I was starting to feel a little bit better about things, but just at that point another elf pushed through the crowd. This one had a long black beard and a dark tunic and big black bushy eyebrows that looked like caterpillars whispering secrets.

Father Vodol.

'No,' he said. 'That's wrong.' And he pointed at me. 'That human there is a threat to us all. My newspaper tells the truth about such matters.'

Captain Soot was beside my feet now. He hissed up at Father Vodol.

Father Christmas stepped in front of me. 'Leave her alone,' he said. 'She is a very good person. Amelia saved Christmas. Don't you remember? She saved it from your plans to destroy it – how you got the Flying Story Pixies to trick the trolls.'

'Ha!' scoffed Father Vodol. 'Christmas! *Christmas!* Well, of course a human would want to save Christmas. Of course a human would want to make sure elves spend their entire lives slaving away making toys for humans to enjoy. What human wouldn't want that? She's a violent, dangerous criminal and she should go back to where she came from!'

I stepped out from behind Father Christmas to see that the crowd was split in half between elves who were nodding their heads and elves who were shaking their heads. Basically, all the Toy Workshop elves and most of the grey-haired elves were on our side, while a lot of the other elves, who had less to do with Father Christmas and the workshop, seemed to be on Father Vodol's side.

But Father Vodol wasn't finished yet. He stood in front of the crowd and spoke in such a loud voice that all the reindeer in the field behind the path looked up. 'She destroyed Kip's sleigh – and not just any sleigh! The Blizzard 360, the highest example of elf technology. Kip worked on that sleigh for a whole year. Every single day. But this isn't important because of the sleigh crash. It's important because of *why* she crashed it. And do you know why?'

'It was an accident,' I mumbled.

'I'll tell you why,' thundered Father Vodol. 'I'll tell you why.' And then he did: 'She was aiming at an elf!'

'Who?' The word flew around the crowd like a bird made of voices.

'You'll find out in tomorrow's Christmas Eve edition of the *Daily Truth*. I have one of my top journalists, Spicer, working on the story. Isn't that right, Spicer?'

And the little blond-haired barrel-shaped elf next to him nodded his head. 'Absolutely, boss. Kip saw everything. It will be the story of the week – if not the century.'

This was just too much. I felt such anger my body seemed to vibrate from the inside. I stepped forwards and stood on the doorstep where all the elves could see me. The whole

crowd fell silent. Mouths fell open. I stared over at Blitzen in the distance and I imagined he was giving me a small nod of encouragement.

'That is an absolute lie. I am very, very sorry that I broke Kip's sleigh. Extremely, absolutely, one hundred per cent *sorry*. But it only happened because I was trying to save my cat.' I picked up Captain Soot at this point, for added effect. 'I had to cut the sleigh free and then the sleigh fell to the ground in the middle of nowhere, over in the Wooded Hills. Kip was nowhere near. There was no way he saw what happened.'

Father Vodol smiled, and walked over to me.

'You see how humans can lie? The question is: who do you believe? An elf like Kip who has lived here all his life? Or a random lying human girl from south of Very Big Mountain who has come to live here for free in the biggest house in Elfhelm.'

Father Christmas was getting a bit red-cheeked with crossness. 'It seems to me, Father Vodol, that you are trying to ruin yet another Christmas. Amelia is *not* a random human. She is a very special person indeed.'

Father Vodol stroked his beard. 'Well, it's always been clear to me, Father Christmas, that you care more about humans than elves.'

'That is simply not true. Elves were miserable when you were in charge. Now they are allowed to sing and spickle dance once more. They have good jobs in the workshop. There is something to work towards. A chance to spread magic. All day today the workshop elves have been brimming with excitement and singing Christmas songs.'

Father Vodol closed his eyes. He clenched his teeth. His forehead rippled and bubbled like water in the wind. Veins bulged below his skin. 'Would anyone like a sneaky peek of tomorrow's newspaper?'

'Yes!'

'Yes!'

'Yes!'

'No drimwickery, Father Vodol,' said Father Topo.

But it was already too late. Drimwickery was underway. And before we knew it, something was flying through the air. Lots of things. At first I thought they were birds, flapping their wings. But they were newspapers – hundreds of newspapers. Each one landed into the hands of an elf, and it turned out there were just enough for every elf there.

Father Vodol looked a little exhausted by his efforts, but he seemed pleased.

Everyone began to read the front page. 'Magic seems to be on my side. I've been struggling with it recently, but elves must be turning. My kind of hope is in the air.'

A newspaper landed in Father Christmas's hands. I saw the front cover. There was another picture of me and this time the headline said: 'MURDERER!'

I began to read the article as Mary joined us on the step.

'What's going on here?' she wondered aloud. And then she gasped as she looked down and saw the newspaper. She began to read exactly what I was reading:

The human girl known as Amelia Wishart did not simply destroy a sleigh. The Daily Truth *can now reveal that this human, currently staying in Father Christmas's extravagant mansion on Reindeer Road, was in fact trying to kill a little elf baby and her mother. Yes, that is right. Bonbon, the sweetmaker, and her baby Suki were the targets of this attack. But fortunately Suki's cries alerted her mother and they ran to safety before the sleigh crashed to the ground.*

Sleigh instructor and former human kidnap victim Kip, who designed the Blizzard 360, saw it happen with his own eyes.

'I saw it happen with my own eyes,' he told the Daily Truth.

Read more about this dangerous human on pages 2, 3, 4, 5, 6, 7, 9, 10, 11, 15 and 17. And read our 24-page pull-out guide: 'What to do if you see a human girl approach you! Apart from RUN and SCREAM FOR HELP – though do that too.'

I had never felt so angry. Not even in the old days, when I had been in Creeper's Workhouse. Nothing had ever made my heart race this fast or make my face feel so hot with rage.

'Look, here's Bonbon,' Father Vodol said, 'and her little baby Suki . . . Tell them, Bonbon, what happened.'

'Well, I don't really know. It was all a blur. I was in the forest looking for some new flavours – berries and such – to get some ideas for sweet recipes. One minute we were just walking along, then the next minute I saw this sleigh heading towards us.'

I felt as if I would explode. But I wasn't the only one who was angry. Because Mary was now storming over to Father Vodol with her pan full of hot Christmassy berries.

'No, Mary, no!' said Father Christmas.

'That would be a bad idea,' agreed Father Topo.

'Uh-oh!' said one of the Sleigh Belles.

Anyway, Father Vodol had no time to do any drimwickery because Mary was too fast. Within a moment she was there, right next to Father Vodol, who – even though a tall elf – only reached Mary's middle. He glanced up at the tilting pan, and then the hot purple fruit began to pour onto his face and hair and beard.

The whole crowd gasped. And then gasped again.

'How DARE you say that about Amelia!' said Mary, who – once Father Vodol was entirely covered with fruit – swung the pan at his head. But Father Vodol, wiping the fruit from his eyes, saw her in time. And he hastily did a little drimwick, and although Mary tried very hard to do some magic of her own to defend herself, her drimwick lessons still weren't going very well, and she froze like a statue.

'See!' gloated Father Vodol, wiping the hot fruit from his face. 'Look how violent and dangerous humans are. Is that what we want in Elfhelm?'

'Unfreeze her this minute!' said Father Christmas. But of course he didn't have to wait for Father Vodol. He was already doing drimwickery of his own. A second later Mary was moving again. The saucepan and the hand that held it kept swinging through the air. But Father Vodol had stepped back now so she didn't hit him. She just kept on going and then twirled around and fell into the snow.

Father Christmas and I went to help her up, taking a hand each.

'It's all right, Mary,' said Father Christmas. 'Don't worry about him.'

Father Vodol snarled. 'Look at them! Looking after each other. We have to be careful. In the space of a year the human population of Elfhelm has TRIPLED.'

Father Christmas laughed. 'Yes. From one to three. And two of us have been drimwicked so we're not technically human at all. Amelia is the only one.'

It echoed inside me like a cry in a cave.

The only one.

The only one.
The only one.

I wanted to head back inside and climb up the chimney and stay there for ever.

'Yes,' said Father Vodol to the whole crowd, many of whom were busily reading lies about me in the *Daily Truth*. 'You are right, I suppose. She is the only one. The only pure human in Elfhelm. And the very worst of all of you. And we know Christmas is nearly upon us, but she is not welcome here.'

'She has nowhere else to go.'

I could hardly think straight. I just kept staring at all the elf eyes looking up at me. Some of them had friendly sympathetic faces and some had unfriendly faces, but it didn't matter. It didn't make a tiny difference. I was not one of them. I couldn't dance like them or do maths like them or make toys like them or ride sleighs like them. Eventually, they'd all turn on me. Maybe even Father Christmas would turn on me. The longer I stayed living with Father Christmas and Mary – Mother Christmas – the longer there would be talk and whispers and gossip, and the gossip would grow.

I had to get out of there.

I couldn't live in a chimney.

There was no escape, so long as I was in Elfhelm.

'There is nothing more to say,' said Father Christmas, 'or to see. It is very nearly Christmas, and that is what we should focus on. Amelia is a good person. I know it as much as I know anything. If you choose to see the good in someone, you will see it shine back. And so it is with her.'

With that, he took my hand, marched us back into 7 Reindeer Road and closed the door quietly.

The Letter Catcher

That night while Father Christmas and Mary were sleeping, I put on as many clothes as I could, and my warmest boots, and I went downstairs to Captain Soot, who was in his basket licking a front paw. I picked him up, filled my pockets full of berries and gingerbread, and crept out of the house as quietly as a mouse.

I left a note on the kitchen table: 'I am heading back to the human world. I belong there. Please don't look for me. Amelia.'

I slipped along Reindeer Road in the dark, seeing the silhouettes of sleeping reindeer, and – even though it was night and a bit scary – I went the quiet way via Quiet Street and Very Quiet Street. I passed the exceptionally small cottage with the black door and one tiny window that belonged to Father Vodol, then crossed quickly over the Street of Seven Curves, heading fast and straight towards Very Big Mountain.

Captain Soot was trembling from the cold. I tucked him inside my coat and held him close.

I began to climb the mountain. It was hard work. My feet sank deeper and deeper into the snow.

'It's all right,' I kept on saying to Captain Soot, but I knew it wasn't at all.

I had no plan other than to keep walking south. Once upon a time, when he was just a boy called Nikolas, Father Christmas had walked all the way from the middle of Finland, from near the small town of Kristiinankaupunki, and he had made it to Very Big Mountain before he'd collapsed in the snow. But I wouldn't have to go *that* far. All I had to do was make it to the first village or town on the other side of the mountain. Someone would surely help a child on their own.

And I had a cat. People like cats.

My legs felt heavier than pine trunks. Now the snow was nearly over my knees. The stars in the sky above me blurred with the tears in my eyes. Eventually I reached the top of the mountain. In front of us, in the dark, I could see miles and miles of forest.

'There,' I told Captain Soot, whose head was peeping out from between two coat buttons.

'That's the human world. That's where we belong.'

Captain Soot gave me a quizzical look.

'All right, I know you aren't a human,' I told him. 'But the human world *is* the cat world. Humans and cats belong together. Well, humans belong with cats. Maybe not the other way around.'

Captain Soot snuggled back into the warmth of my coat.

Then, suddenly, I heard a voice, calling out in the dark. I looked around. The voice wasn't coming from behind me. It was coming from slightly higher up, right at the pointed peak of the mountain.

'Hey! You there! What are you doing?'

It was a high-pitched voice. An elf voice. *Oh no.*

I struggled to see in the dark but whoever it was was coming closer. Despite his short legs and despite the deep snow, he was fast. He seemed to be a very acrobatic elf, like someone you would find at a circus. He didn't so much step through the snow as hop and skip and leap over it. Then he finished with a massive triple somersault and landed on a rock that was sticking out of the snow, right in front of me.

The elf had a broad smiling face and wore a long hat – even longer than a normal elf hat – with a thick furry brim. It was a special hat – a snow hat – made for the kind of elf who expected to be outside a lot. I also noticed he had a massive rucksack on his back.

'You must be the human girl!' he said.

Uh-oh, I thought. *Here we go. Another elf who believes Father Vodol's lies.*

'Just leave me alone, okay? You stay with the

elves. I'm going back to the humans where I belong.'

The elf kept smiling, even though his eyes looked a little sad. 'Well, okay, but I thought it would be nice to have a chat. Because it's quite lonely up here, on top of Very Big Mountain, with no one to talk to. You see, elves generally like company. Conversation. Hanging around in crowds. You've probably noticed.'

I thought of all those elf eyes staring at me when I had been standing on the doorstep. 'Yes, yes, I've noticed that . . . but the truth is I wouldn't be much fun to talk to right now.'

The elf pressed his finger to his chin. 'Well, what about *now*? I mean, you said *right now*. But the thing with nows is that they are all different. Now. Now. Now. There is always a different now happening, if you think about it. This now is different to that now, which is different to that now – the one where I just said now. The trick is to know how to catch them.'

I was confused. This was a very confusing elf. But I supposed it was better to be confused than horrendously SAD in capital letters, which was how I had been feeling before I'd felt confused.

'Do you know what *isn't* hard to catch, though?'

'What?' I asked.

The elf was suddenly jumping into the air – diving, doing another somersault – right over my head. When he landed on the snow, even though the snow was very deep, he hardly made an impact. He had perfected the art of the light landing.

And then he held up something in front of me. Something white in the moonlight.

An envelope. 'Letters!' he said. 'Letters are easy to catch. Well, for me. It's my job you see.'

'You're the Letter Catcher?'

'Yes, I am. All the letters that humans write and send to Father Christmas make their way here. They float through the wind, pushed along by the wishes they contain, and there are thousands every day. From all over the world. And they all make it here, to Very Big Mountain, because . . .' Just as he was saying this, he spotted another letter flying past his face, and he reached out and grabbed it. 'My name is Pippin. Pip for short. Pleased to meet you.'

'I'm Amelia.'

'Amelia. Amelia. A-ME-LI-A. It sounds nice. It sounds like a . . .'

Captain Soot suddenly peeped out from my coat.

Pippin jumped in the air in shock. 'Aaagh! You've got two heads! No one told me human children have two heads!'

'This is a cat,' I said.

'A what?'

'A cat. He belongs on the south side of the mountain. Like me.'

Pippin placed the two letters in his rucksack. 'But what about Father Christmas and Mother Christmas? You live with them now, don't you?'

I sat down on the rock sticking out of the snow. I nodded. 'I did, but it hasn't really worked out.'

'Why? Is Father Christmas cross with you?'

'No, but he should be.'

'Why?'

And so, right there, on top of Very Big Mountain, with the whole of Finland spread out in front of me, I told Pippin everything. And about my plan to return to the world of humans.

'So you were always happy there? In the human world?'

I shook my head. 'No, not always. Not even

often. But at least I *belonged* there. At least I didn't get anyone into trouble but myself. The elves don't want me here.'

'That's not true. Lots of elves want you here. I was *so* excited when I found out that a real-life human child was living in Elfhelm. It was amazing.' And then he looked up into the sky and behind him. 'Oh, that's peculiar.'

'What is?'

'Look at the sky. Look at the Northern Lights.'

I stared up at the faint billowing green waves of light in the sky, sprinkled like magic dust. 'They're there every night, aren't they?'

'Yes, but not like this. Normally they fill the whole sky and are bright, illuminating the whole of Elfhelm. But they're dimmer tonight. They're hardly there at all.'

'What does that mean?'

'It means there isn't as much magic in the air. Which is probably why there are fewer letters reaching here than normal.'

I didn't really understand what this meant, but as I stared down the snowy Finland side of the mountain I noticed something land in the snow nearby. Another letter. Pippin had noticed it too.

'That is even peculiar-ier. I know that isn't a word, but if it was, it would be it.'

'Why?' I wondered. 'What's so weird? I thought you said letters fly up here all the time.'

He nodded. 'Yes! They do, they fly up *here*. Not down there. Ever since Christmas the letters have been making it right to the top of the mountain. In the old days, two years ago, it was a different story, but recently things have been

going super well. Sometimes I even have to jump up *higher* than the mountain to catch them.'

He jumped up high, with his right arm stretched up into the sky, to show me what he was talking about.

Pippin then stared at the letter below him. 'There's another one. Look, just beyond it.'

He leapt down – no somersault this time – and hopped and ran through the snow, picking up both letters.

He came back up to where I was still sitting, opened one of the letters and read it out.

Dear Father Christmas,

My name is Elias. I live in the town of Linköping in the country of Sweden. I would very much like a pack of cards for Christmas, so I can play games with my sister, who has been very poorly recently. Thank you for coming to visit us last year. We loved the spinning top and the bouncing balls. Our year has been so much more magical simply knowing you came and will visit again. So thank you a million times.

Very best wishes,
Elias (aged nine)

As Pippin was reading I thought of the letter I had once written to Father Christmas, when I had lived at 99 Haberdashery Road in London. I remembered thanking him and telling him all about Captain Soot – *he sometimes steals sardines from the fishmonger and gets into fights with street cats* – and then I had got on with the main business of the letter. The wishing part. I had asked for four things:

A new brush for sweeping chimneys
A spinning top
A book by Charles Dickens (my favourite author)
For my mother to get better

Of course he couldn't do anything about the fourth one. That was the whole problem. That made me angry with him for a while, before I understood that magic has to have limits for it to *be* magic. Before I worked out that magic doesn't take away all the bad things – it just makes it easier to get through the bad things knowing that life can contain magic, and that it will contain it again.

I was thinking all this as Pippin folded the

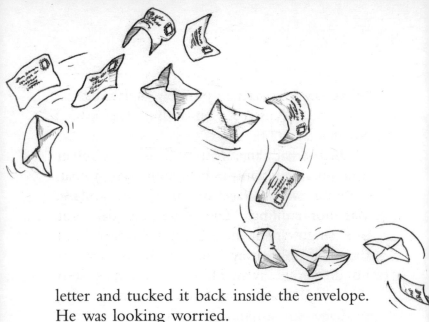

letter and tucked it back inside the envelope. He was looking worried.

'Sweden,' he said. And he kept saying it, almost as a question. 'Sweden? Sweden? Sweden?'

'What's the matter?'

'The letter was from *Sweden*.'

'And?'

'Well, Sweden is close. There is Finland and then there is Sweden. The countries are joined together. Letters from Sweden are *always* the highest.'

Then he looked at the back of the other envelope. 'Norway.'

He placed his rucksack on the ground and looked at all the envelopes, sometimes opening one to read the address on the letter itself.

'Finland . . . Finland . . . Norway . . . Finland . . . Sweden . . . Russia . . . Finland . . . Finland . . . Sweden . . .'

'Well, what's the matter?' I asked, Captain Soot purring warmly as he slept inside my coat.

Pippin, whose face was made for smiling, was not smiling. 'The matter is that not one single letter here comes from over a thousand miles away. Not even from over five hundred miles away.' He dug really deep into the rucksack and pulled out some more. 'Ah, this one is from India. And this one is from America. And this one is from Scotland. That's more like it . . . But those letters from far away were from hours ago. None of the letters arriving *now* are from any of those places. They're from nearby countries. They don't need as much magic to get here. So, if letters from far away can't get here now, it means something is happening. I think there's an energy crisis.'

'An energy crisis?'

'A hope crisis. A diminishing of now's. That's why the letters aren't getting here. And why the ones that do aren't reaching the top of the mountain. It's why the Northern Lights are fading . . .'

'But what's caused it?'

'I don't know. Something recent. Tonight. And it's serious, because you know what today is? It's Christmas Eve Eve. All the letters have to get here by tomorrow.' He looked around, then up at the sky, then towards the dark forests of Finland, then back to the small dots of cottages in Elfhelm, before his big eyes turned to me. '*You.*'

'What?'

'It's because of you.'

I felt sad. 'You see? I told you I didn't belong there.'

Pippin was shaking his head and wagging his finger at the same time. 'No, no, no. Don't you get it? You have it the wrong way around. The hope levels rose when you arrived here. And they are diminishing because you're leaving. Think about it. If you go now, Father Vodol wins. He'll get his revenge. A lot of elves will believe what he tells them. They'll think human children are evil. Even the workshop elves might start to think it. And as soon as they think that, they'll not want to work for Father Christmas. And if they don't work for Father Christmas, then poor little Elias from Linköping and all the other millions of children around the world won't have any presents in their stockings – or magic in their lives.'

I thought about this. And as I thought, Pippin took some gingerbread out of his pocket and broke it in two and offered some to me.

'I am telling you,' he said, between crunches, 'that if you went down that mountain and never came back here, the Northern Lights would fade. And there would be no letters to catch.'

'Well, that would be good for you.'

Pippin choked on his gingerbread. He shook his head and jumped to his feet. 'Are you *kidding me*? This is the best job in the world. Sure, it can be lonely sometimes, but I am literally catching dreams. I am the bridge between two worlds. I am making Father Christmas happy. Before I was a letter catcher I worked in media sales.'

'Media sales? What's that?'

'Ugh! It was the most deadly boring job in the whole of Elfhelm. It was for the *Daily Snow*. Back when it was full of lies – when Father Vodol ran it. Anyway, Father Vodol is a very greedy elf. He wanted to fill the newspaper with adverts, so it used to be my job to wander up and down the Main Path, going into all the shops – Mother Mayhem's Music Shop and Clogs! Clogs! Clogs! and Red & Green and Magic Books – and I'd get them to buy adverts in the newspaper. But the trouble was Father Vodol used to want them to sign these things called *contracts*, and elves aren't very good with contracts, so they'd sign them because it seemed like a fun thing to do, you know, writing their signatures in big letters – I used to carry lots of multi-coloured pens in my pocket – but they didn't know what they were signing. For instance, the Figgy Pudding café ended up agreeing to a whole year's worth of adverts. They closed down because they owed Father Vodol all their money . . . Now, of course, the *Daily Snow* hardly has any adverts at all, because Noosh is a nice elf and she doesn't believe in people signing their names on pieces of paper that they don't understand. She wants to make money from people buying the newspaper, but no one seems to want to buy it.'

'Because she wants to tell the truth.'

'Yes.'

Captain Soot woke up and I fed him a little crumb of gingerbread.

'But how can I stay if everyone hates me?' I asked.

'Well, you are not the only one everyone has hated, you know. When I worked in media sales, all the elves hated me too. I would try and cheer them up with acrobatics. I would spin and flip and somersault down the Main Path, but they didn't care so long as I had contracts in my hand. And they didn't care that I had little elves at home to feed. But then, when I started working for Father Christmas, he saw a different Pippin. He saw the good in me, and he saw my leaping and acrobatics and he knew just the job for me.'

'Letter catching.'

'Exactly. But if you leave, there won't be any need for a letter catcher. There won't even be a need for a Toy Workshop or for Father Christmas. You could save him. You could save us all from Father Vodol taking over again. If you leave now, I guarantee that just after Christmas Father Vodol will be Leader of the Elf Council again. And all the happiness of Elfhelm will be gone – this time for ever. And no human child will have a Christmas present ever again.'

Captain Soot licked his lips. He liked

gingerbread. I stroked him as I tried to think. 'But what can I do? He can write whatever lies about me he wants. If I stay, then I'll be the most unpopular person ever to live here. And, if Father Vodol takes over, he will open up Elfhelm prison again and probably lock me up. And he might lock Father Christmas and Mary up too, simply for being humans.'

'So you have to stop him.'

'How?'

'By doing something good. By . . . doing something good and *showing* elves that you are here to help us, not to hurt us.' He took off his hat to scratch his head. 'If you scratch the right part of your head, the ideas jump out, you know. But it has to be the right part. It can't be just any part.' He tried different parts of his head – top, back, behind each pointed ear – and I scratched my head too, to see if it worked for humans as well.

'A-ha!' he said, leaping into the air. 'I've got it! You pay back the sleigh!'

I sighed a cloud of cold air. 'I've already thought of that. But how? I'm no good at elf jobs.'

'Well, what are you good at?' asked Pippin.

'Writing, I love it,' I said.

'You should work for the *Daily Snow*! You should write the most amazing story that will make people want to read the *Daily Snow* again.'

'I've thought of that too. I even talked to Noosh about it. But truth can never beat lies. It's impossible.'

Pippin pressed his finger to his lips. 'Sssh! Don't say that word. Truth can be more magical than any lie in the world. If Father Vodol takes over again, if he gets into the hearts and minds of all the elves again, all hope will be lost. And no hope means no Christmas. Ever again. There would be a hole inside me I wouldn't be able to fill.'

I stared out – not at Finland's forests this time, but in the other direction. At Elfhelm. In the moonlight and soft faded glow of the Northern Lights I could see it all. The village. The Toy Workshop. Reindeer Field. And there, to the west, the Wooded Hills where the pixies lived and where I had crashed the Blizzard 360. Somewhere, amid all of Elfhelm and those hills, there would be a story. An amazing story that Noosh and elf readers would love. One that would give them hope again. But what?

And then I realised what Pippin had been saying. 'Say that again,' I told him.

'Okay,' he said, shrugging. 'Truth can be more magical than any lie in the—'

'No, not all of it. The last bit, the last thing you said.'

'There would be a hole inside me I wouldn't be able to fill.'

A hole.

I stood up from the rock. On top of the mountain. There, at the exact point between the world of humans and the world of magic. 'That's *it*,' I said.

'What's it?'

'The hole. When I crashed the sleigh I saw a hole in the ground. The hole obviously led somewhere. It was there for a reason. There was a Flying Story Pixie and he spoke of paper birds flying out of it. Paper birds. They won't really have been birds. They'll have been newspapers. I've seen them fly. Father Vodol makes it happen. With his dark drimwickery. I'm going to explore it. I'm going to go into the hole and find out why it's there. I'll find out what Father Vodol is up to . . . *That* could be my story.'

'Sounds a bit dangerous,' said Pippin, looking worried.

But just then he pointed to something

I couldn't quite see – on the human side of the mountain. 'Look!'

And then I *could* see it. An envelope floating and twisting through the night air. And, unlike the two envelopes I'd just seen, this one kept going, up and up and up, right to the top of the mountain, and even higher – so high that Pippin had to jump as high as he could. He caught it. He smiled as he showed it to me. 'Look! Queensland, Australia! That's the other side of the world! Hope is back in the air! And look! Look at the sky!'

I stared up at the night sky. It was bursting with the most luminous green.

'You must be on to something!' Pippin shouted.

And I felt excited and terrified all at once.

I took a deep breath and looked towards Elfhelm, with Captain Soot snug in my coat, I stared towards the darkness of the Wooded Hills and wondered what awaited me there. I had only taken a few steps down the mountain when eight reindeer and a large sleigh appeared, galloping on the air towards me.

'It's Father Christmas!' squealed Pippin excitedly.

And it was.

The sleigh skidded to a halt in the air, inches above the snow, right in front of me.

'Amelia! Where have you been?'

'I'm sorry,' I said. 'I thought I didn't belong. I thought I was making everything worse. I thought you and Mary were better off without me. I was trying to go home.'

'But, Amelia, we are your home. Me, Mary, Reindeer Road. That's where you belong.'

And it felt so nice to hear him say that, I just climbed into the sleigh and put my head on his warm shoulder, saying goodbye to Pippin, but not mentioning a single word about Father Vodol or my plan.

A Deal with the Truth Pixie

ather Christmas took me home. I went to sleep. I woke up. I had breakfast. I acted totally sorry for sneaking away, and then – when Father Christmas and Mary left for the workshop – I sneaked away again. But this time, I knew exactly what I was doing. And my first stop was the Truth Pixie.

'So, as it's Christmas Eve, we need to be clear. I get half the money but you do all the work?'

The Truth Pixie – arms crossed, mouse in pocket, leaning against her door – drove a hard bargain, but I needed her.

There was no point in simply finding an amazing story. Whatever story I found, Father Vodol would simply say it was a lie. And Noosh had been very clear – I had to *prove* everything. And there was no better way to prove something was true than to have a Truth Pixie confirm it was so.

'Yes,' I said, 'that's right.'

'And will you write about me too?'

'Absolutely.'

'And Father Christmas will read it?'

'He will indeed. It will be a Christmas present to him.'

'And you'll go first? Into the hole?'

'If you really want.'

The Truth Pixie nodded and held out her hand. 'It's a deal, Round Ears.'

Into the Tunnel

An hour later we were at the hole. It was dark but it was shallow. I stood with my feet at the bottom of it and with my head sticking out above ground level.

Hmmm, I thought to myself. *Maybe there isn't much of a story, actually.*

But when I crouched down inside the hole I realised that it wasn't just *one* hole. It was a hole that led to other holes.

'There are seven other holes – tunnels – all around the side of this one,' I told the Truth Pixie. 'Smaller ones.'

I looked into each of the seven tunnels. They were all as dark and mysterious as each other. There was no way of knowing which one would lead to something interesting. Maybe they all would. Maybe none would.

The Truth Pixie peered over the edge. 'Ah yes, well, they all look too small for you to fit inside, so I guess that's your story: "Holes discovered in forest. Realising they were too small to fit inside, I went home."'

'I can fit inside them. And if I can, so can you.'

'No way! They're far too small for a giant freak like you. And for me too. Maybe a mouse could fit inside, but I left Maarta at home, so . . .'

'Well, I used to sweep chimneys, and some chimneys were a lot smaller than this. Come on, let's try this one – the one heading east towards Elfhelm.'

'I don't know . . .' the Truth Pixie said nervously.

I looked her in the eye. 'When Father Christmas finds out you helped me, he will be so impressed.'

'Will he?'

'Yes, he will.'

And so she followed me into the tunnel. We crawled on our hands and knees in the dark

for ages, until the light behind us disappeared altogether and the darkness became total. It was very tight in the tunnel, especially for me, but once I got into a rhythm I could crawl along on my elbows quite quickly.

Pretty soon, the tunnel gave us a choice. We could go left, or we could go right. The tunnel to the left felt slightly larger than the one to our right, so we went left.

'Our chances of not being crushed to death are slightly better this way,' advised the Truth Pixie helpfully.

But then there was another choice. And we chose right. And then left. And then, at a kind of tunnel crossroads, we went straight on. And then left. And then right.

The Truth Pixie sighed. 'I believe we are now lost. Which means our chances of dying underground have greatly increased.'

'Please, do you have to say that?'

'It's the truth.'

'But you could also be silent, couldn't you? If you're silent, you aren't lying. You're just being silent.'

'I always talk when I'm nervous. It reminds me I'm alive.'

I had never known dark like the dark of

those tunnels. People think chimneys are dark but chimneys aren't *totally* dark. There is always some light from below and above, and when you have spent a lot of time in chimneys you can see things. You can put your hands in front of your eyes and see your fingers. But in the tunnels I couldn't see my fingers. I couldn't see anything at all.

'What is it like?' came the Truth Pixie's voice, from behind. 'Living with Father Christmas?'

'Well, I'm struggling to fit in, you know, in Elfhelm and—'

'I don't care about Elfhelm. What is *he* like? What does he do? You know, in the house?'

'Erm, well, he eats a lot. And cooks.'

'Does he sing?'

'Sometimes. Sometimes he sings.'

'What does he sing?'

'Christmas songs.'

'So predictable – and yet adorable . . . Has he ever mentioned me?'

I couldn't really remember but I wasn't a Truth Pixie so I could be diplomatic. 'Oh, I don't know. Maybe. Yes, I'm sure he thinks of you a lot.'

'What does he say?'

'Oh, probably things like "I really like the

Truth Pixie. The Truth Pixie is great. Ho ho ho.'"

'Ho ho ho? Why does he say that?'

'He always says that. It's how he laughs. Most people go "ha ha ha" or "hee hee hee". But Father Christmas goes "ho ho ho". It's a rounder way of laughing.'

'So he laughs at me.'

'No. He laughs when he's happy, which is most of the time.'

'He's such a weirdo,' said the Truth Pixie dreamily. 'A big, round, laughing, utterly adorable, gingerbread-scented weirdo.'

We kept crawling and crawling and crawling. After a long time (maybe an hour, but it was hard to tell) the tunnel led into another one. A larger one. A *lighter* one. Little worms glowed. Magic worms. Multi-coloured worms. Yellow. Green. Indigo.

'Colour Worms,' the Truth Pixie said, 'which is strange.'

'Why?'

'Because Colour Worms aren't earth worms. They're tree worms. You find them in trees, and in books. But books and trees are the same thing. My aunt used to tell me that books are just trees that are having a dream. She was a Dream Pixie, not a Truth Pixie, and while Dream Pixies tell a bit more truth than Lie Pixies they go for the most beautiful explanation of things rather than the real one. So my aunt used to say that the moon was always on its own in the sky because it had fallen out with the sun, and that the moon often felt sad, and when it got sad it became smaller and smaller, so when you saw a crescent moon it was the moon being quite sad indeed, and when you saw no moon at all it was impossibly sad. And she also said that was where snow came from. From the moon, flaking away. But, anyway, my point is that Colour Worms never live below ground. Not naturally.'

'So how did they get here?' But even as I asked the question I guessed the answer, the one the Truth Pixie was already whispering urgently.

'Someone put them here. So they could light the tunnels.'

'But who?'

'The same people who built the tunnels in the first place.'

We came to another turning, where we had to choose between two directions.

'Let's go the lighter way,' I suggested. 'And look, this tunnel's a bit wider.'

'No. No way,' said the Truth Pixie. 'That's where the tunnel builders will be.'

'*Exactly*. And that's why we *should* go there. We should go and see who they are. This is our story – this way. Come on. Let's go.'

She reluctantly followed me as we kept crawling, mindful not to accidentally squash any of the Colour Worms that lit our way.

And then I noticed something. A footprint. No. A paw print. I stared down at it. A round circle with four smaller ones – toe prints – just above it. There was another one right beside it.

The Truth Pixie squeezed in beside me and looked at

it too. And she quickly pointed out other footprints in front of us.

'Uh–oh,' she said. 'It's rabbits.'

'Rabbits? From the Land of Hills and Holes?'

'Yes. But it's two hundred miles away. So these tunnels must be two hundred miles long.'

'Or maybe,' I said, thinking aloud, 'the rabbits travelled over ground all the way to the Wooded Hills, then dug that hole.'

'Maybe. Or maybe there are other holes. Maybe these aren't ordinary holes. Maybe they are to release something. Or maybe they are traps. Maybe we are going to be bunny breakfast.'

'Could you try and be a bit more positive?'

'I am a Truth Pixie. I have to be truthful about every possibility. I can't just bury my head in the ground. Not until a rabbit stamps on it. Not until . . .' And then she stopped. I could see her face, illuminated in a whole rainbow of colours from the bright worms sliming around us. She frowned, trying to concentrate. The pointed tips of her ears twitched.

'Uh–oh.'

'What is it?'

'Can't you hear it?'

'Hear it? Hear what?'

But then I heard it too.

Something up ahead. Something very faint, but growing.

Not voices. But a kind of whooshing. A kind of flapping.

'We need to run,' said the Truth Pixie. 'We need to run VERY FAST and VERY QUICKLY and VERY NOW.'

But we couldn't run. This tunnel was made for crawling, not running. And even if it had been it would have been too late.

Because they were coming towards us.

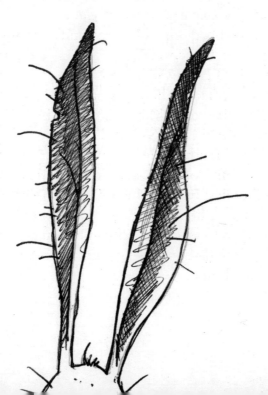

'Birds!' I shouted. 'Get down!'

But the Truth Pixie not only had sharper ears she also had sharper eyes. 'They're not birds.'

And the Truth Pixie – being the Truth Pixie – was right. We lay as low as we could on the tunnel floor as a thousand flying things flapped over us.

Paper. They were made of paper.

I remembered the flying newspapers landing into the elves' hands. I also remembered what the Flying Story Pixie had said, with his silk-smooth voice, that day I discovered the hole. *Once upon a time, there was a paper bird . . . Flying out of a hole and into the light.*

I grabbed one of them and saw my own face on the cover. There it was, beneath the words 'THE DAILY TRUTH'. But it wasn't just my face. There was a picture of Father Christmas and Mary too. The headline was 'HUMANS MUST GO!'

The Truth Pixie saw it and scowled. She read some of the words in the article. 'This is full of lies! Father Christmas doesn't hate elves! Father Christmas does not secretly want humans to take over Elfhelm! Father Christmas does not have millions of chocolate coins stored in his house!'

'He certainly does not,' I said.

The paper was now pulling away, out of my hands, and I let it go. It joined the others, flying through the tunnel and probably heading out into Elfhelm.

We carried on. The tunnel was getting brighter and more colourful because of ever increasing amounts of Colour Worms crawling in and out of the soil all around us, and it was getting wider and wider all the time, so now we could crawl side by side.

'This must be where Father Vodol is printing the newspaper,' I said. 'Father Christmas was wondering how he was making newspapers, now he doesn't have the *Daily Snow* building. This must be how.'

'But Father Vodol is not a rabbit,' observed the Truth Pixie. 'And we saw rabbit paw prints and not elf paw prints. Because elves don't have paws.'

'That is indeed the truth.'

'It certainly is. But these rabbit tunnels aren't big enough to hold a printing press or a newsroom. Unless . . .'

'Unless?'

We waited a moment in silence. The Truth Pixie's ears twitched again.

'What now?' I asked.

'Voices. Listen . . .'

And I listened. But I couldn't hear anything at all. Although I could *smell* something.

Something rather nice too.

Chocolate!

'The voices are coming from that way.' She pointed to the path glowing to our right. That was where the smell of chocolate was coming from too.

'What kind of voices?' I asked.

'I don't know. And, to be honest, I don't want to find out. I want to go back.'

'We need to stick together,' I told her. 'Listen, something is going on here. Something major. Rabbits, flying papers, underground tunnels. A scent of chocolate. This is weird. Father Christmas could be in danger. Do you want to run away from helping him? Or do you want a chance to be his hero?'

The Truth Pixie, still on her hands and knees, looked at me with a pained expression. 'I want to help him. I want to be his hero. I want him to dream of me the way I dream of him. I want him to say "Truth Pixie, I don't know what I would have done without you."' She looked cross after she had said all this. 'Now, please, no more questions. If you ask me a question, I have to answer it. I physically can't leave a question hanging in the air. I have to tell the truth. I have to say it out loud. It's terrible.'

'The truth can never be terrible.'

'It can *always* be terrible,' said the Truth Pixie. 'And I should know.'

I headed towards the smell of chocolate and reluctantly she followed. Soon enough I was hearing the voices too. It was probably another five minutes after that when we reached the opening. It wasn't an opening *up* though. It was an opening *down*. We could see a glowing, in the distance, rising from below. The path stopped – or rather sloped suddenly downwards, steeply – and we could see a vast underground room or hall or *burrow*.

And that is where the rabbits were.

Hundreds and hundreds of rabbits. Thousands. A whole army of them.

Only these were not ordinary rabbits that you could fit inside a small hutch. No, these rabbits were all as large as dogs. Big dogs. Each as tall as a pixie. Some even the size of elves. And they were all standing on their hind legs in this large underground space, a space

illuminated not just by Colour Worms but by the fire of lanterns hanging all around. And these rabbits wore clothes. Army clothes. Combat gear. Tattered. Blue-and-white coats with gold buttons. Many of them – the ones near the front who might have been generals – were wearing black hats. The kind of hat Emperor Napoleon had worn. Some of them had gold medals stitched to their chest pockets.

There was a vast copper tank that looked like a giant soup pan standing amongst the rabbits.

All the rabbits had their backs to us. They were staring towards a little one in a tall black hat and a red coat. Although he was smaller than the rest, even on his hind legs, he was higher than them because he was standing on a kind of stage made of earth. His ears were very long and stuck up, though his left one flopped a little. He was walking back and forth, talking as loudly and clearly as his big front teeth allowed.

I lay down as close to the edge as I could and peeped over.

'What are you doing?' the Truth Pixie asked me, in a whisper so quiet it was hardly louder than a breeze.

'I'm watching,' I whispered back. 'This is our story. This right here.'

The Truth Pixie rolled her eyes, but stayed there with me, pressed to the ground, as we watched and listened, our hearts beating so hard they could almost have given us away.

'Oh no,' came the Truth Pixie's tiny whisper. 'I know who that is.'

'Who?'

'It's the Easter Bunny!'

The Easter Bunny

The Easter Bunny paced around the stage, looking very serious and grumpy by rabbit standards.

'Look at us,' the Easter Bunny was saying to the crowd. 'Look at us here. War generals. Soldiers. Geniuses. Artists. But underground. Unseen, being rabbits. Hidden away from daylight, from the world. We have for too long been the underclass.'

'Too long,' muttered much of the crowd in agreement. 'Too long.'

'And look at what we have done. Look at what we are capable of. We are geniuses. Look at this warren. We create a vast network of tunnels wherever we go!' He pointed to the copper vat in the centre of the room. 'We managed to get *that* in here! And we beat the trolls at the Battle of the Underground Cave!'

'Yes, we did!' said the rabbits.

'But more than that, we are *artists*. Those elves above us may be good at making things – toys, sleighs, all that basic stuff – but what

we do is *art*. The intricacy of our tunnels. The joy of our music. The craftsmanship of rabbits like my poor long-lost mother and her incredible chocolate egg sculptures. We have the souls of poets. What we have is imagination. But we are also warriors! And we know why we have to be. We are under threat, once more. The elves and the humans are joining forces. The elves have a new hero. A fat grey-haired man in bad clothes who goes by the name of Father Christmas. And there are other humans there too now. And they clearly plan to take over all the Magic Lands. But we are not going to let all our efforts become sidelined. No way. We are rabbits! And not just any rabbits! We are the rabbits of the Land of Hills and Holes. We aren't going to take it any more.'

'We aren't going to take it any more!' agreed the rabbits.

The Easter Bunny laughed. He had the craziest laugh I had ever heard. He tilted his head back and almost howled. It was like a rabbit doing an impression of a wolf. But then, halfway through, the laugh became softer and sadder and faded quickly into nothing.

When the laugh stopped, he looked around the vast burrow. He looked up. For a heart-stopping moment I thought he could see us, peeping over the edge, but then he said, 'I would now like to introduce someone to you. A very special guest. He is an elf, but don't hold that against him.'

The rabbits all seemed to talk at once.

'Stop your rabbiting!' said the Easter Bunny. 'And put your paws together for the only elf you can trust . . . The elf we have worked alongside in our new warren . . . Father Vodol!'

So it was true. Father Vodol *was* at the heart of this. The Truth Pixie and I could hardly breathe as we watched the black-bearded elf walk onto the stage.

'Thank you, Easter Bunny,' he said, smiling. 'And thank you, rabbits. Thank you for letting me use the space next door. It might not be quite the newsroom my staff and I are used to, but it does the job. And speaking of doing the job . . . well, TOGETHER we are going to do the job of stopping Father Christmas. We have the same aim. I need to stop the elves being brainwashed, and you need to make sure you can live without the fear of humans taking your lives. That means making sure we STOP Christmas! And stop FATHER Christmas!'

The crowd cheered.

'And the way we do it is by showing the whole of Elfhelm that rabbits and elves – despite our history – are natural friends. And humans are the opposite. We have to show them that *we* are on the side of truth. And the best way to do that is to lie.'

The Truth Pixie gasped beside me. Some of the rabbits looked confused.

Father Vodol continued: 'Directly above us is the Bank of Chocolate. And inside the bank is . . . well, a *lot* of chocolate.'

So that was where the delicious smell was coming from.

'The finest chocolate you can find anywhere. And it will all be yours. Yours! We will fill the huge tank with melted chocolate and you can make the most exquisite egg sculptures anyone has ever tasted. And there will be no chocolate coins in any children's stockings this year. And no elves will get paid for all their hard work in the workshop. And they will get angry, and they will want someone to blame . . .'

The Easter Bunny was nodding at all of this, his drooping left ear becoming vertical with interest at what he was hearing. And then he stepped forwards again and placed his paw on the elf's back. 'And they *will* have someone to blame, won't they, Father Vodol? Tell them. Tell them.'

'Father Christmas,' said Father Vodol. 'Father Christmas will be known as a bank robber.'

The Easter Bunny bit his paw with excitement. 'You see! It's what I've been telling you all! Easter will be back. Christmas will return to what it used to be: a miserable, grey, cold winter day. And Easter, the time of rabbits rising from the ground in glorious sunlight, will once more be the time that people care most about. Sorry, Father Vodol . . . do go on.'

Father Vodol cleared his throat. 'The *Daily Truth* will tell the story of the bank robbery and get it into every elf's hands.' The Easter Bunny's eyes were as wide as plates with excitement as he listened and nodded. 'And that's not all. There is a *motive*. Father Christmas has been struggling for money and everyone knows it, thanks to a certain newspaper that has been flying out of rabbit holes. Yes. He wants to pay for a sleigh that the horrible human girl destroyed. So he is the most likely person in the whole of Elfhelm to rob a bank. It's utterly perfect. And then, after that, Father Christmas will be sent to prison, and I will become Leader of Elfhelm once again, and you rabbits will be free to enter Elfhelm and live there as you see fit.'

'He's evil,' whispered the Truth Pixie. 'And the rabbits can't see it.'

She was right. The rabbits were cheering. And the Easter Bunny was now at the front of the stage again.

'Thank you, Father Vodol,' said the Easter Bunny, clutching hold of a pendant hanging around his neck. 'It is time for Christmas to be forgotten. It's time to make Easter great again . . . Now, everyone, I have a question.'

'Oh no,' the Truth Pixie said. 'Not a question. Not a question. Not a question. Cover my ears.' She quickly put her hands over her ears. I knew why. The Truth Pixie had to answer questions truthfully, for the asker to hear. She couldn't help it. She was a Truth Pixie. So I clamped my hands over her ears – or rather, over her hands over her ears – hoping she wouldn't hear the Easter Bunny's question.

But the Easter Bunny raised his voice, and the words boomed around the vast burrow. 'Someone, give me an honest answer. What do you think of Father Christmas?'

And I could see from the Truth Pixie's eyes that she had heard. Her large pixie ears were, after all, super sensitive.

There was a deadly hush throughout the warren. Not a single rabbit spoke, but all their ears were vertical as they listened out for the first answer.

'Anyone?' asked the Easter Bunny. 'Come on, don't be shy. Answer the question. What do you think of Father Christmas?'

The Truth Pixie winced, and held her breath, and turned crimson, knowing she was going to answer the question. She desperately tried to cover her mouth, but her hands burst suddenly away, and she just couldn't stop herself shouting it out at the top of her voice for the rabbits and the Easter Bunny and Father Vodol to hear.

'I THINK HE'S WONDERFUL!'

A gasp spread through the burrow like a wind. Everyone looked all around, trying to locate the echoing voice.

'Who said that?' demanded the Easter Bunny, quick as a flash.

The Truth Pixie was now desperately trying to press her hand over her mouth, but the hand simply refused to do it, even when I pushed it too. It was like trying to join the wrong ends of powerful magnets together.

'I SAID THAT!' she yelled, despite herself. 'ME, THE TRUTH PIXIE!'

'Ah!' said Father Vodol. 'The Truth Pixie! I know who this is. Ask her anything! She'll have to tell you!'

'Where are you?' shouted the Easter Bunny. 'Who are you with? What are you doing here?'

'Sssh!' I told the Truth Pixie.

But of course it was no good.

'WE'RE UP HERE! I'M WITH AMELIA, THE HUMAN GIRL! WE'RE SPYING ON YOU! AND NOW WE'RE GOING TO RUN AWAY!'

The Easter Bunny looked up and caught sight of us. 'Look! There they are! Imposters! Rabbits, get them! Bring them to me!'

And then we started to crawl back through the tunnel. As fast as we could.

'I'm sorry!' the Truth Pixie squealed.

'It's not your fault,' I told her.

221

'I hate it when I do that!'

We took a left then a right, down a tunnel we hadn't been down before, simply because it was large enough to run inside, and quite dark, with hardly any Colour Worms. But then we heard it. A kind of rising thunder that shook the ground we were standing on and made little clods of earth fall onto our faces. It was the charge of a full Rabbit Army.

'Run!' said the Truth Pixie. 'Run! RUN!'

But it was no good. We had no idea where we were going. The rabbits knew the tunnels far better than we ever could.

'Oh no,' I said, seeing shadows in the darkness ahead of us. 'We've got to turn back! We've got to go the other way!'

So we did – and immediately saw rabbit shapes coming towards us. Some running, some hopping, some scurrying on all fours. The one closest to us, we could now see properly. She was wearing a tatty green army jacket complete

with medals, and had an eye-patch. She was carrying a big net attached to a long stick.

A second later we were inside it. Inside the net. Being dragged away.

'Good work, 382!' one of the rabbits said to our captor.

'We need to escape!' I said, grappling with the net as we were being hauled back towards where we had just run from.

'There is no way,' whispered the Truth Pixie. 'There is no escape.'

And, of course, it was the truth.

A Lesson on How to Love Life

y the time we were back in the vast underground burrow it was already happening.

A thick stream of chocolate was rushing down, like a waterfall, from the middle of the ceiling, straight into the large copper tank.

We watched, aghast, restrained by 382, our captor, and another, both with knives at their belts. 'You see,' said the Easter Bunny. 'See that? Up there? That hole where the chocolate is coming from? It goes up for about a mile. That's how far below the bank we are. We did that. Do you know how difficult it is to build tunnels straight *up*? With nothing below you?'

'No,' said the Truth Pixie wearily. 'I don't know that. It must be very difficult I would imagine.'

'Yes, very difficult. But my rabbits are the best of the best. Maybe even the best of the best of the best. I wouldn't go so far as to say they are the best of the best of the best of the best, but they are very good indeed. And they did that.'

'You'll never get away with this!' I wailed.

And then Father Vodol stepped forwards. 'Oh yes, we will. Especially now that you have made our jobs a whole lot easier.'

I stared down at the furry paws that were holding me tight. 'What do you mean?'

The Easter Bunny stared at my face – a face which was probably full of fear and hatred, because I was feeling a lot of those things. Fear. And hatred.

'What have you been told about me?' he asked, and I could tell that the question was specifically for me and he genuinely wanted to know. And even though I wasn't the Truth Pixie, I told him the truth. After all, I had nothing to lose.

'I know how you and your army drove out the elves from the Land of Hills and Holes. I know that you took lots of elf lives. I know that you used to live below ground, then one day wanted to live in the open. I know that you destroyed the peace.'

'You can keep quiet, you know?' whispered the Truth Pixie. 'You aren't *me*.'

The Easter Bunny stared at me, and looked at the rabbit holding me, the one with the eye-patch who had captured us in the net.

'You see, 382? You see the lies they are told. You see how even the truth is pushed underground . . .' Then the Easter Bunny came close to me, whiskers twitching and curling at their ends. It was hard to tell what he was thinking. At first I thought he was angry, but when I looked into his eyes I saw nothing but sadness. A sudden, dark sadness. 'It was the *opposite*. We were always above ground, as soon as the weather became a bit less cold, around Easter time. We wanted to live peacefully with the elves. We had once lived in Elfhelm, before it was called Elfhelm. And it was the elves who drove *us* away. I bet no one ever told you that. We were forced to move. We were good and peaceful creatures. And that's the real story.'

The Truth Pixie sighed. 'I hate to say it but he seems to be telling the truth. I have an instinct for spotting a lie, as you know, and I'm pretty sure he hasn't told one.'

'But if you are good and peaceful creatures, why would you do this? Why would you capture us? Why would you rob a bank?'

The Easter Bunny sucked his teeth. 'The key word is *were*. We *were* good and peaceful creatures. Past tense. But that did us no favours at all. If we had stayed good and peaceful creatures then we wouldn't be here now. None of us would be here now. Rabbits had to change. *I* had to change them. We couldn't have gone on the way we were. Not if we wanted to survive.'

'But it's always better to be good.'

'Oh, I used to think that too, but I saw my own parents end up in a pot. They ended up as a stew, for trolls! Good is overrated. It's better to be alive. It's better to be free . . . and that freedom is under threat again. Father Christmas is going to keep bringing more and more humans into the Magic Lands. And do you know what humans do to rabbits? They eat them. Just as trolls ate my ma and pa.'

'Well, I've never eaten a rabbit,' I protested.

'And neither have I,' said the Truth Pixie, trying to resist the grip of the big burly floppy-eared rabbit soldier who held her. 'Like most pixies, I'm vegan.'

The Easter Bunny was hardly listening to us. He seemed to be lost in his own memories. His eyes looked as close to crying as rabbit eyes can get. He looked, for a moment, soft and vulnerable – the way rabbits are supposed to look.

'They used to be sculptors. Well, Ma was. She sculpted chocolate. She was an artist, really.' He held up his pendant. It was a shining jewel, like a diamond. And inside it, there was something else. Small. No bigger than a thumbnail. Brown. Egg-shaped.

'What do you think that is?' he asked us.

'Is it a rabbit dropping?' asked the Truth Pixie. 'It looks like one. A big one.'

'You have to excuse her,' I said. 'She can't help it.'

'It's an egg. It was the last thing my mother gave me. This small chocolate sculpture. She called it simply *Egg*. She said it was meant to represent how life is fragile and delicate – the egg – but should also be enjoyed – the chocolate. You see, it's art. A chocolate egg. It's a lesson on how to love life. Every lesson we need. And it was for me.' He sighed a long, sad sigh. 'And I've kept it ever since.'

'It's beautiful,' I said, and it was. A perfect egg made of chocolate.

'I was good, you know,' he said softly. 'Everyone thought of me as good. I used to like that . . .'

Father Vodol, beside him, patted the Easter Bunny on his back. The rabbit almost flinched at his touch. 'Yes, well, you still are good. But you can't just let people walk all over you. You have to shine. You have to get out there, above ground, and make people fear and respect you. Unless you want every rabbit to crack like an egg underfoot.'

The Easter Bunny stood up straight. 'You are right, Father Vodol. You are right.'

'Now we have the girl, our plan is even more perfect. She can go and tell everyone in Elfhelm that the reason no one can get their money out of the bank this Christmas Eve is because Father Christmas – dear, jolly, kind, ho-ho-ho-ing Father Christmas – is in fact a thief.'

'I will never say that. And no one would believe it anyway.'

'Oh, I think they would. Do you have any idea how many times Father Christmas has been at the Bank of Chocolate this month? Trying to borrow money to help repair the sleigh you wrecked. And if anyone doesn't know, they will soon. It's covered at length in today's evening edition of the *Daily Truth*. And we've already got the headline for Christmas Day. Follow me.' He stared at the rabbit holding me. 'I want to show her something. You don't mind, do you, Easter Bunny?'

'Not at all. I'll come with you.'

So I was led away, away from the Truth Pixie, to a nearby underground room.

Anger boiled inside me. And then it kept boiling as I saw, there in the rabbit burrow, an underground newsroom, complete with some elves I recognised.

'Spicer! Come here. Give us the mock-up for our Christmas Day special.'

And then Spicer, that barrel-shaped elf with

the oversized tunic I had seen in the crowd
on Father Christmas's doorstep, came over with
a sheet of paper that showed the Christmas
Day front page.

'There you go, sir.'

Father Vodol showed it to me. It was nothing
but a headline in huge black letters.

'FATHER CHRISTMAS–BANK ROBBER,'
I read out loud.

And that is when my anger bubbled over and came out of my mouth. 'You can't do that!'

'You know what, Spicer, I think she is right,' said Father Vodol. 'We shouldn't run with that headline.'

Spicer seemed genuinely confused. 'Shouldn't we?'

'No. We should put it in speech marks. "FATHER CHRISTMAS – BANK ROBBER – says the human girl".'

'I will never say that.'

'You just did! And you will again.'

'Okay, okay,' said the Easter Bunny. 'Please don't think we're evil. Try to see the bigger picture. Now, let's get things moving. Some of my rabbits will accompany you above ground. And Father Vodol, of course. And then Father Christmas will be locked away.'

Father Vodol's smile curled like a snake. 'For ever, this time.'

'But I'll tell everyone you're lying.'

He didn't even blink. 'Oh no, you won't, because if you do that your little pixie friend will end up very, very dead.'

'Incredibly dead,' added the Easter Bunny, with sad eyes. 'As dead as a chocolate egg.'

Father Vodol gazed at me for a moment, his skin glowing from that strange light of fire lanterns and Colour Worms. 'Right. Let's go. Let's stop Christmas.'

The Bank Robber

There was chaos on the Main Path. Outside the Bank of Chocolate elves crowded around to listen to what Sovereign was telling them.

'It appears we have been robbed,' she said, clasping her hands together, smiling a professional bank clerk smile. 'There is no more chocolate in the vault. Which means of course there is no money we can give you.'

'But it's Christmas Eve!' one elf said.

'And it's payday!' said another.

They hadn't seen us yet. It was just Father Vodol and me now. The Easter Bunny was waiting inside Father Vodol's house on Very Quiet Street. I had just left there. You see, one of the rabbit tunnels, the one we entered via the underground newsroom, led straight into Father Vodol's tiny living room. There was a ladder and everything. So each time anyone saw Father Vodol enter his house, they were really seeing him enter his vast new secret newsroom.

Anyway, the Easter Bunny was staying there

and we were not too far away, around a couple of corners, on the Main Path, heading towards the commotion. Father Vodol was carrying a toy whistle, the kind made in the Toy Workshop. He had told me what it was for. If he gave one sharp blast, then the Easter Bunny would head quickly back down into the warren and give the order for the poor Truth Pixie to be killed.

They hadn't explained exactly *how* they would kill the Truth Pixie, except by chocolate. Maybe they were going to plop her into the hot liquid chocolate lake and leave her there.

The one thing I did know is that they were serious. One blow of that whistle and the Truth Pixie would be in trouble.

'Are you ready?' said Father Vodol.

'No,' I said.

'Too bad.' And then he raised his voice. 'What's going on here?'

The elves all turned to look at him.

Pi was there. 'There has been a bank robbery.'

'Oh no!' said Father Vodol, faking surprise. 'I wonder who could have done that?' He turned at me and kept nodding his head. 'Amelia! You look like you want to tell us all something.'

'Do I?'

'Yes, you absolutely do.'

'I don't think I do.'

All the elves were staring at me. Many were holding their latest copy of the *Daily Truth*. I saw Noosh in the crowd. She was frowning at me, and already seemed to know something odd was going on.

'Amelia, tell the elves what you just told me.' He opened his hand and showed me the whistle. 'In the next five seconds, ideally.'

He pinched the whistle between his thumb and forefinger and lifted it slowly to his mouth. In five seconds he was going to blow the whistle. In five seconds the Easter Bunny would hear it and head down into the burrow with the Truth Pixie. She would die. Whatever happened I had to stop Father Vodol from blowing that whistle.

'Four . . . three . . . two . . . one . . .'

'All right!' I shouted, just as the toy whistle reached Father Vodol's lips. 'All right! I know who did it!'

'Who?' asked Mother Breer.

'Yes,' said Sovereign, 'you must tell us. Who is the bank robber? If you have information you must give it.'

I took a deep breath and could hardly believe what I was about to say. 'It was Father Christmas.'

Gasps spread among the crowd.

Voices grew.

'I knew it!'

'He's been having money problems recently.'

Noosh stepped forwards with Little Mim. She stared at me incredulously. 'That's impossible. That is a total lie.'

Another gasp from the crowd.

I stared at the whistle, hanging in Father Vodol's mouth. I had to make them believe me. The Truth Pixie's life depended on it. 'It isn't. It's true, I'm afraid.'

'But it makes no sense', said Noosh. 'Father Christmas is a good person. He has worked his whole life trying to make people – elves as well as humans – as happy as can be. He simply could not do this.'

And then I thought of something. If Father Christmas was going to end up locked away, then he was not going to be locked up alone. After all, this was all my fault.

'I did it too. I was involved.'

I watched the elf faces. Obviously these were not the elves most loyal to Father Christmas

– most of them worked in the Toy Workshop and would not be out on the Main Path on Christmas Eve – but, still, to see their once friendly faces so angry and hateful was quite scary, and reminded me of the mob that had crowded around 7 Reindeer Road yesterday evening.

'Why are you lying?' Noosh asked me. 'Listen, everybody, Father Christmas and Amelia are not bank robbers.'

Father Vodol pulled the whistle from his mouth and put it back in his pocket. 'No wonder you can't sell any newspapers with such foolishness as that, Noosh. Don't you understand? Father Christmas didn't give himself a pay rise because he wants to look *good*. He wants everyone to love him. Elves, humans, the entire world. It's pathetic! He's an egomaniac! And a liar! And, as of today, a *bank robber*!'

'Lock him up!' someone shouted.

'Lock him up!' said someone else.

'Lock him up! Lock him up! Lock him up!'

'Now,' said Father Vodol, 'we need to do something very quickly. This situation can't go on. As the last proper Leader of the Elf Council before Father Christmas it falls upon me to take charge of the situation. Now, he's not going to give up easily. He'll expect all those loyal foolish elves busy now at the workshop to keep working all Christmas Eve . . . EVEN THOUGH HE HAS STOLEN THEIR MONEY!'

'He hasn't stolen their money,' said Noosh, and I wanted to say it too, but couldn't. And, anyway, her voice was drowned out by the crowd.

'Listen,' said Father Vodol, quietening everyone down. 'It is very likely that Father Christmas is planning his escape this very night, when he flies into the human world. And he will take all your money with him! Unfortunately, the elf army was disbanded when he first took over, but luckily I have a solution.'

'What's that?' asked Sovereign.

'Rabbits,' he said. And then he shouted the word as loud as he could. 'RABBITS! RABBITS! RABBITS!'

The crowd stared at him, mouths open, bewildered.

'We are on the brink of an all-out war with humans . . .' said Father Vodol.

'We're really not,' attempted Noosh. But it was no good.

'Rabbits are our only hope of protection. In my first act as Emergency Leader of the Elf Council I hereby declare the Easter Bunny and the Rabbit Army to be our new allies in the defence of Elfhelm from the corruption and trickery and selfishness of humans.'

'That is a truly awful idea,' said Noosh.

But it was already happening. I could see the Easter Bunny, followed by his army of rabbits, marching towards us.

'Aaagh!' wailed Little Mim, pulling on Noosh's hand. 'Rabbits!'

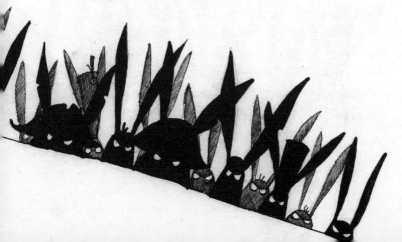

'Take Amelia into the warren and keep her there!' said Father Vodol, once they had arrived.

'Don't you dare!' protested Noosh.

'One more word out of you, and you and Little Mim will be sent there too.'

Noosh pulled a terrified Little Mim tighter to her, and she began to cry for me as I was dragged away by two rabbit soldiers.

I could hear Father Vodol in the background. 'Now, don't worry, elves. The Easter Bunny and I are here to help. We and the Rabbit Army are going to head straight away to the Toy Workshop and bring Father Christmas to justice.'

And, as I was hauled away back through Elfhelm, towards Very Quiet Street and the warren below, I kept thinking about Father Christmas right at that moment. There, in the workshop, holding open his infinity sack as all the elves queued up to drop the presents they had made inside. I knew he would be so happy. This was his favourite day of the year. He would be singing. The whole workshop would be too. And then, right about now, there would be a knock on the door. And the Rabbit Army would enter. As I headed back into the darkness of the warren, I didn't have a thought for myself. I just kept on thinking of Father Christmas's smile fading as he came face to face with the Easter Bunny, and then being arrested and dragged to the underground prison that I was now headed towards.

I felt so guilty I could have cried. But I didn't. Crying wasn't going to save Christmas.

In the Cages

There was a prison, in the warren. There were no Colour Worms. Just flickering lanterns and four human-sized cages – or 'hutches', as the rabbits called them. I was in one of the hutches. Father Christmas was in another. And the Truth Pixie was in a third. The bars of the hutches were so close together even a pixie could not squeeze through. There was one empty cage at the end that soon had a new occupant. Two rabbits, on Father Vodol's orders, brought a very confused Mary into the warren and pushed her inside.

'What's going on?' Mary asked.

Father Christmas explained. 'They think I robbed a bank. They think you all helped.'

'And it's my fault,' I said.

'Yes, it is absolutely her fault,' said the Truth Pixie.

Father Christmas tried to reach through the bars of the cage for Mary's hand. 'I'm sorry about all this, Mary. It's not—'

'No,' I interrupted as three rabbit guards stood watching us, sharing a carrot between them. 'The Truth Pixie is right. This is all my fault. I'm sorry I have ruined Christmas.'

The Truth Pixie, by the way, was the only one of us who for the moment didn't seem worried. 'Just like the old days, FC? Father Vodol locking us up together. It's destiny, don't you think? We're meant to be together.' She stared at Mary, who was glaring at the pixie. 'Sorry, Lumpy.'

'My name is Mary.'

The Truth Pixie shrugged. 'I never said it wasn't.'

'We've got to get out of here!' said Father Christmas. 'It's Christmas Eve! Children all over the world are expecting me.'

The Truth Pixie sighed. 'You know, maybe you should just give up on the whole Christmas thing. It seems to bring you a lot of unnecessary trouble.'

Father Christmas ignored her and started to talk to one of the rabbit guards – the number 555 stitched onto his jacket. 'Listen, furry friend, ever so sorry to bother you but we really need to get out of here quite urgently. I have a lot of work to do tonight. I know you have orders to follow, but it's Christmas and that is the time of year for, you know, tipping things upside down, subverting the established order, doing something unexpected, and being *good*.'

555 ignored him and kept munching on his carrot.

'What's going to happen to us?' I asked.

The Truth Pixie shrugged. 'Bad things, I'd guess.'

'What about magic?' I whispered, when it

looked like the rabbits weren't paying attention. 'Drimwickery. If you can fly around the world and stop time, then surely we can escape an underground rabbit hutch?'

'I would love to think so, Amelia,' replied Father Christmas, 'but you are forgetting something. Magic depends on hope. What hope do we have? There is no magic in the air, not down here. There is no magic among the elves. Even some of the workshop elves will have turned against me, now they think I am a bank robber.'

'They won't think that, sweetbread' said Mary, looking at him fondly. 'Father Topo will be telling them the truth. Come on, we need to find some hope.'

The Truth Pixie was shaking her head. 'Father Topo won't know the truth.'

'Well, he'll know Father Christmas isn't guilty, just as Noosh does,' I suggested.

'It won't be enough. Elves aren't pixies. They aren't free thinkers. They tend to believe what they read in the papers.'

I had never seen Father Christmas like this before. There was no twinkle in his eyes. No smile on his face. His cheeks looked distinctly un-rosy, and he was sighing heavily. 'Father Vodol has wanted this day for years. And now it is here. It will be a disaster for the elves. They will become scared and miserable and unkind, the way they once were. And it will be a disaster for humans too, because now there will be millions of empty stockings all around the world. It will probably be a disaster for Father Vodol too, even though he doesn't realise it yet. And there is nothing we can do about it. Even if we get out of this prison we'd still have the whole Rabbit Army against us, and every elf who chooses to believe the *Daily*

Truth. It's . . .' He stopped. He couldn't believe he was about to say it. 'It's . . .'

Mary was shaking her head and sniffing quietly.

And then he said it. Father Christmas said the word I never thought I'd hear him say.

'It's *impossible*.'

Death by Chocolate

And just at that moment we heard voices coming through the tunnel. Our guards stopped munching their carrots and stood to attention and saluted as the Easter Bunny and Father Vodol marched in.

The Easter Bunny came up to the cage containing Father Christmas. His nose and whiskers twitched. His dark eyes glistened gold from the reflected lantern flame. 'Well, well, well, the famous Father Christmas! Global celebrity! The most popular person in the world. And yet, here you are. On Christmas Eve. In a rabbit hutch. Under the ground. I'm guessing you won't be so popular tomorrow, will you? When all those excited children wake up early and open their limp little stockings to see nothing but – well – *nothing*. You'll be the most unpopular man of all time.'

'Why are you doing this? I have never done anything to you. I have never even thought of you.'

The Easter Bunny closed his eyes suddenly as if he'd been slapped. '*Never even thought of me?* Of course not. The arrogance of Christmas right there. The arrogance of humans. Well, let me tell you, you don't think about us because we are like Easter itself. We are too complicated for your simple brain. You want toys and shiny baubles and annoying songs. We are rabbits. We believe in the complexity of life. We believe in art. And we will fight for it. And you don't think of us because you don't understand us. It's just the way everyone always wanted it. Keep the rabbits underground. Out of sight. Out of mind.'

Then Father Vodol stepped forwards. 'And now it's time for the humans to be underground. To be out of sight and out of mind.'

He stroked his beard as if it were a cat. I suddenly thought of Captain Soot. I wondered if he was still in the house. I hoped he was safe. I wished I was with him.

'Right now,' continued Father Vodol, 'right at this moment, at Really Quite Late in the Day, on Christmas Eve, the Toy Workshop is empty. All the workers have been told to leave. They are now in the village hall, where some senior generals in the Rabbit Army and some of my own journalists are explaining the situation.'

'Explaining the situation?' huffed Mary. 'You mean *lying*?'

Father Vodol ignored her. 'Now, talking of explaining the situation, we should say a little about your situation, shouldn't we, Easter Bunny?'

But the Easter Bunny looked a little distant, and didn't appear to be listening. He was busy comparing his grubby red army jacket with Father Christmas's immaculate bright red coat. 'It's really red,' he mumbled.

'All right,' snarled Father Vodol. 'I'll explain. You are now deep, deep under the ground. This is, apparently, the lowest part of the whole warren. Now, you see that tunnel over there?' He pointed to one of the three tunnels that led here.

'We see it,' said the Truth Pixie.

Father Vodol gave a quick nod. 'Well, it's actually more of a chute than a tunnel. You see there's just too much chocolate, and the

rabbits are going to need another place to store all the melted chocolate. To hide it. And this place is very, well, *hidden.* A hiding place inside a hiding place. So this will be the chocolate depository for now. This place here is just big enough. The chocolate will fit perfectly. We will tip the container over, towards the chute, and it won't take long to fill. The delicious chocolate will rise up quickly and within no time at all you'll be covered from head to toe. Then, eventually, the chocolate will harden and set. By then you will be finished. And no one will ever know. Imagine that. Your bones will be hidden in a block of chocolate until the end of time.'

'What a way to go, eh?' said the Easter Bunny. 'Death by chocolate.'

Impossible Things

The Easter Bunny and Father Vodol had left us.

We were alone – waiting to hear the sound of liquid chocolate rushing towards us.

'We are probably going to die,' said the Truth Pixie.

'You don't know that,' I said. 'You can't know the truth about the future.'

'I said *probably*. It is statistically very, very likely. And that's pixie mathematics. Which make a lot more sense than the elf kind.'

And then Mary, in the cage furthest from me, looked suddenly alert. 'I just heard something!'

'It's probably the chocolate,' sighed Father Christmas.

'No, it isn't. It's a . . . it's . . .'

I heard it too. A cat's miaow.

'Captain Soot!' I shouted as he trotted out of one of the other tunnels.

'Oh, that poor dear horse,' said the Truth Pixie.

Father Christmas rattled the bars of his cage. 'He needs to get out of here!'

'Shoo! Shoo, Captain!' I urged. 'You've got to get out of here. I told you to stay in the house. Go back to the house. If you stay here, you'll drown in chocolate.'

'Shoo!' we all kept saying. 'Shoo! Shoo! Shoo!'

But Captain Soot wasn't going anywhere.

'Right. We've all got to find a way out of here,' I said, with new urgency.

And then Father Christmas said that word again: 'It's just *impossible*.'

I hated hearing it. I realised now why it was a swear word. 'No, it's not.'

Captain Soot was outside my cage. Rubbing the side of his head against the bars. Ridiculously, he was purring. He had no idea of the danger he was in.

Father Christmas stared at me, his face glowing softly in the lantern light. 'You were right all along, Amelia. Some things simply are impossible.'

'It's not impossible,' I told Father Christmas. 'Come on.

Say it. An impossibility is just a possibility you don't understand yet.'

'Amelia's right,' said Mary. 'Remember? We thought we would stay trapped in that workhouse for ever.'

'Well, now you are trapped in a cage underground,' observed the Truth Pixie unhelpfully, 'and facing almost certain death. That is not really great progress.' But then she remembered something. 'Father Christmas, can you remember your first chimney? Can you remember that tiny little hole in the roof of that prison in the tower? You were ten times the size of that chimney. And you did it. You escaped. And it was the most wonderful thing I have ever seen in my life.'

Father Christmas smiled with a kind of pride. 'I have travelled through chimneys smaller than that. I have even travelled through chimneys that aren't even chimneys. And you don't get much more impossible than that.'

'Well, then,' I said, 'you can do it. You can get us out of here.'

'I can do anything with hope in the air. But there is no hope in here.'

'It's Christmas Eve!' I told him. 'The whole *world* is hoping.'

Father Christmas closed his eyes. 'I can't feel it in here. We are too far under the ground. And there is obviously no hope in Elfhelm. And we are *way* below the Northern Lights.'

'It has to come from us,' I said. '*We* have to hope. If we all hope, then we might just get out of here before the chocolate floods us.'

Father Christmas considered. 'Something impossible needs to happen. That is the quickest way to conjure hope. Belief in impossibility. And to believe in the impossible you sometimes need to see it.'

I closed my eyes. I thought of my mother. How, after she died, I had imagined nothing good or fun would ever happen in my life again. And how I had been wrong. Life hadn't been perfect in Elfhelm. But now I realised that I'd had a lot of fun. Ice skating. Trampolining. Eating delicious berry pies. Playing elf tennis after school with Twinkle. Sure, school had been hard, but a lot of people found school difficult. And life at home with Father Christmas and Mary and Captain Soot had been a joy. And I'd never thought joy would have been possible.

'You saved my life,' I told him. 'I believe in you.'

'You saved mine too,' said Mary, staring hard at her cage door.

The Truth Pixie was trying to find something positive to say too. 'I pretend my pillows are your belly. And I place my head on them and think of you.'

And this made Father Christmas laugh, but when he stopped laughing we heard it. The rushing, whispery noise that could only mean one thing: the chocolate had been sent down the tunnel and was pouring towards us at terrifying speed. And we could smell it too. That wonderful – but now very scary – smell of pure delicious chocolate.

'Here it comes,' said the Truth Pixie.

'Oh no,' I think I said.

'Miaow,' said Captain Soot.

'We need more hope,' said Father Christmas.

And Mary said nothing at all. She just seemed to be concentrating very, very hard.

It happened quickly. The chocolate flooded in. Within a second it was around our ankles. And touching Captain Soot's tummy.

'Captain!' I said desperately, clapping my hands. 'Get out of here. Leave us!'

Clap! Clap! Clap!

And the chocolate kept rising and rising and

rising. Captain Soot was now swimming in it as it rose over my knees, to my waist.

'Drink it!' suggested Father Christmas, who still couldn't find the drimwickery inside him. Drimwickery that was badly needed. 'Drink as much as you can.'

So we all started gobbling as much of it as we could. Everyone apart from Captain Soot, who knew just a taste of chocolate could kill him. But you can't instantly consume a whole bank's supply of chocolate. There was just far too much of the stuff. And it was now at my neck. And I looked at the Truth Pixie, who was doing a panicky kind of breast stroke in fast tiny circles. As the chocolate lifted me off my feet, I saw Father Christmas still furiously gobbling chocolate. Mary, though, looked totally calm, with her eyes closed, even as it reached her chin.

And then it went totally dark – completely utterly pitch-black – as the lantern flames were extinguished.

I raised my hand up and now I could touch the hutch roof above me. Getting closer and closer.

This was it.

'We're going to die,' said the Truth Pixie.

And I knew she was right.

It really was impossible to escape now.

I even said the word. Or started to.

'There's no hope. It's impossi—'

But things can change in a moment. Things can change in the space of a word. Between the third and fourth syllable, *everything* changed.

One moment I was about to drown in melted chocolate deep underground, and the next I was lying on a street, soaked from head to toe in chocolate, out in the frosty air. A street sign said: 'VERY QUIET STREET'.

I realised where I was. I was outside a simple wooden elf cottage with a tiny window and black door. Father Vodol's house. I could see Captain Soot, also drenched in chocolate, shaking it off his paws. Then another chocolate-smothered figure – the Truth Pixie – sitting up beside me on the street and scratching her head.

'Well, this is peculiar,' she said.

And then the door was flung open and I could see Mary – red-faced and puffing and clenching her teeth – carrying – yes, *carrying* – Father Christmas. She laid him on the grass beside us.

He smiled a big chocolatey smile. 'What happened?' he asked her.

'I finally found it. I finally found magic.'

'You got through the cage? You stopped time?'

'I did the . . . *impossible*, yes.'

Father Christmas beamed. 'Those drimwick classes were worth it in the end! You've saved us all!'

'Even me,' said the Truth Pixie. 'Thank you, Lump— I mean, Mary.'

'Yes, I suppose I did.' Mary chuckled and wiped the chocolate off her face.

And Father Christmas got to his feet and

hugged her, and gave her a chocolatey kiss.

'That is disgusting,' grumbled the Truth Pixie. 'I think I might actually throw up.'

I stood up and saw that it was getting dark. It wasn't over yet, I realised. We were seen as criminals. There was Father Vodol and the Easter Bunny and the entire Rabbit Army and a lot of angry elves against us. There were still our lives and our freedom and a whole Christmas to save.

'We need to get to the Toy Workshop!' said Father Christmas. 'Now!'

And we all started to run there – leaving lots of brown footprints behind us.

A Hidden Humdrum

This feels so wrong,' said Father Christmas, looking around at all the discarded toys in the empty workshop. 'Christmas Eve. And not a single elf here.'

'I-I-I'm h-h-here,' came a voice.

Father Christmas recognised it instantly. 'Humdrum? Where are you?'

The nervy elf crawled out from under the table with all the spinning tops on it. 'I'm here, Father Christmas.'

'What happened?'

'Well, after the rabbits took you away some of them stayed and told us you had robbed the bank. I knew it was a lie. Every elf in here knew it was a lie. But we were told to leave. They were all sent to the village hall. They had no choice.'

'But you're still here.'

'I h-h-hid.'

'That was a very brave thing to do, Humdrum,' said Mary.

'Very brave,' I agreed.

'Miaow,' added Captain Soot.

'You need to get out of h-h-here,' said Humdrum. 'All of you. They're going to come back.'

'That is a very good idea,' said the Truth Pixie enthusiastically, stepping backwards out of the workshop. 'Anyway, this has been a really fun day. But I nearly died – twice – and I don't want to risk a third time. So, if it's all right with you, I'm just going to retreat to my humble little home in the Wooded Hills and have a bath. Wash all this chocolate off. I'm sure Maarta's been missing me.'

'No,' I said. 'You can't go. Not yet.'

Those pixie eyes widened. 'I am pretty sure I can.'

'We need you.'

'But I *really* need a bath, so—'

Father Christmas knew what I was thinking, because now he was saying it too. 'Amelia is right. We do need you, Truth Pixie. Just for one last thing.'

The Intruders

When we marched into the village hall – following Father Christmas, as he flung the door wide open – every elf turned around, in a wide-eyed and stunned silence.

Father Vodol, with the Easter Bunny by his side, was halfway through a speech. 'And so I will work together with the rabbits, to help restore law and order to Elfhelm, and make sure that Father Christmas and the other humans can never fool us again. We will, from now on, believe the truth and—'

The rabbit soldiers, standing around the edge of the hall, all looked our way too. I recognised one of them, and caught her eye.

'INTRUDERS!' shrieked 382.

And now Father Vodol was looking with wild, desperate eyes at our chocolate-covered clothes as we approached the stage.

'Look at them! Covered in chocolate from the bank. That's the proof right there. They did it. Can't you see the truth with your own eyes?'

'Truth,' said Father Christmas coolly. 'It's an interesting word. A lot of people use it in different ways. But the truth is *always* the truth. Fortunately we have brought the Truth Pixie with us. And, as all of you know, the Truth Pixie can only tell the truth. So, Truth Pixie, could you tell us who was behind the bank robbery?'

'Oh no,' said the Truth Pixie, as all the elves

and rabbits stared at her, waiting for the answer. 'This is awkward.'

'Tell them the truth.'

Father Vodol stormed to the front of the stage and tried his best dark drimwickery to silence her. But, as all the elves knew, there is no magic in the world that can stop the Truth Pixie from telling the truth.

'Father Vodol and the rabbits robbed the bank,' she blurted. 'The humans are innocent. Father Vodol and the Easter Bunny just wanted them out of the way. That's why we are covered in chocolate. They were trying to drown us with it, in the warren they've built under Elfhelm.'

The whole hall gasped.

'It's true,' said a voice in the crowd. We turned to see Noosh standing there. 'I went inside the bank to investigate. Under the vault there's a hole leading under the ground to a warren. And it's full of chocolate.'

'F-F-Father Vodol is lying to us,' agreed her husband, Humdrum, standing next to me. 'He has always been lying to us.'

'Can I go now?' asked the Truth Pixie.

Father Christmas shook his head. 'No. I have one more question. Did Amelia crash the sleigh deliberately? Was she trying to hurt someone, as Father Vodol told us in the *Daily Truth*?'

'I saw her on the very day it happened, and she told me all about it. And even though I can't tell a lie, I can spot them better than any pixie who ever lived. And I can tell you it was an accident. Amelia is a very good person – kind of annoying, and she gets me into all kinds of trouble – but she would never want to hurt an elf.'

'I knew it!' said Mother Breer. 'She's a good girl!'

'That's what I've been saying!' said Pippin, the Letter Catcher, with the last of the Christmas letters bulging out of his pockets.

'I love humans!' said Little Mim.

There was a massive commotion now.

The rabbit soldiers were waiting for their orders to act, but the Easter Bunny was standing, speechless, next to Father Vodol.

'SILENCE!' screamed the black-bearded elf. 'SILENCE! It doesn't matter who robbed the bank, the humans are a danger to us all.' Then he shouted at the rabbit soldiers as he pointed to us, 'Capture them!'

The rabbit soldiers did nothing.

'I knew that Easter Bunny was evil!' said Mother Miro.

'He always was!' said Columbus.

I stared at the Easter Bunny. He looked bewildered, as if the goodness inside him was still there and trying to come out, but he didn't know what to do about it. I remembered something Father Christmas had told me. *If you choose to see the good in someone, you will see it shine back.*

'No!' I said to the elves. 'The Easter Bunny isn't evil.'

'Amelia!' Mary laughed. 'What are you talking about? He and Father Vodol just tried to kill us.'

'Yes, but he didn't start off that way. The rabbits were good. They were peaceful before the war with the elves.'

'See!' shouted Father Vodol. 'Listen to her anti-elf propaganda. She hates you all!'

'No,' I said, 'I don't. There is nothing to fear from the truth.'

And then the oldest elf in the room stepped forwards. The one with the long wispy white moustache. Father Topo. Everyone listened as he spoke to me.

'Amelia,' he said, 'I am probably the only elf here who can remember seeing the last battle with the rabbits, all those hundreds of years ago. I was only six years old at the time but what I saw shamed me and has shamed me ever since. The cruelty some elves showed on that day was terrible. It is the reason I have always tried to be different to that kind of elf. To be welcoming to outsiders. That is why, once, when I was climbing the mountain with my daughter Noosh, I decided to do a drimwick spell on a dying human boy – a boy called Nikolas, who would eventually become this man you see before you.' He pointed at Father Christmas, who was smiling and wiping a warm tear from his eye. 'It was because I never wanted to fear outsiders. Now, Father Vodol can't remember the old wars. Maybe if he had seen what I had seen his whole attitude would be different. But I want to tell you two things, Easter Bunny . . .'

'What things?' asked the Easter Bunny, holding his pendant, his droopy left ear becoming alert with interest.

'First,' said Father Topo, 'I want to tell you not to trust that elf you are standing next to. Father Vodol only cares about one person in this room, and that is himself. And the second thing I want to tell you is that I am sorry for what happened to the rabbits. We should never have forced you off your land. It wasn't right. And I believe if every elf in this room knew the true story, they would feel the same.'

The Easter Bunny didn't know what to say. His mouth opened, but no words came out.

'What's the delay?' Father Vodol asked the rabbit soldiers. 'Seize the humans! What are you waiting for?'

'Me,' said the Easter Bunny. 'They are waiting for me. They don't take orders from elves.'

Father Vodol's bushy eyebrows rose and fell furiously, like the flapping wings of a dying bird. 'Well, you order them!'

'*I* don't take orders from elves either, as it happens.'

And that seemed to shut the elf up.

Father Christmas went to the stage and faced the Easter Bunny. 'We need to be at peace. I am sorry that you were forced out of Elfhelm. I would like to say, as Leader of the Elf Council, that you and your rabbits can live here in peace. What would it take for that to happen?'

Every elf and human and pixie and rabbit in the room waited in total silence.

The Easter Bunny glanced down at this pendant.

And then I remembered what it contained. The little chocolate egg his mother had given him.

And I had an idea.

'You don't have to hide away any longer,' I said. 'The whole world could know about you, the way they know about Father Christmas. The whole world could know the true message of the rabbits from the Land of Hills and Holes. The message of your parents. Of your mother. About how fragile life is, but how it is to be enjoyed. The message of the chocolate egg.'

The Easter Bunny gazed at me. When he wasn't trying to kill someone, his face was surprisingly kind.

'I don't understand,' he said.

'You're not the only one!' said Mary.

'You could give chocolate eggs to the world the way Father Christmas gives presents,' I explained. 'And no outsider would be a threat to you or the rabbits. They would see your goodness. And we could help you. You could borrow Father Christmas's sleigh and reindeer at first . . . You could work together at Christmas. Children could wake up to presents in their stockings, and eggs wherever you would want to hide them.'

'Could he now?' asked Father Christmas, looking a little miffed. But then he remembered the seriousness of the situation. 'I mean, yes. Absolutely. Of course he could.'

And then the Easter Bunny got it. His eyes glistened. '*The message of the chocolate egg.*'

'Don't fall for it!' said Father Vodol, somewhere between fear and fury. 'As if they mean it!'

'They mean it,' said the Truth Pixie.

But the Easter Bunny was now shaking his head. 'No.'

My heart sank.

And every rabbit soldier looked ready to attack. 382 even had her net out

'It can't be at Christmas,' said the Easter Bunny. 'It's Christmas tomorrow. I'd need more time. It needs its own day.'

And then I had the most perfectly obvious idea. 'Easter? The time of year rabbits head out into the outside world. That's why you're called the Easter Bunny, right?'

'Yes. Yes, it is.' And that was the first time I'd seen the Easter Bunny smile. 'Easter! That would be perfect.'

I smiled too, and so did Father Christmas and Mary, and Father Topo, and the Truth Pixie, and Noosh and Little Mim and Humdrum and Pippin and Mother Miro and Sovereign and Bonbon and Mother Breer and Mother Jingle. And soon all the elves were smiling, even Columbus (although his was a very confused smile, as he kept thinking of all the history books that would need correcting). Even the rabbit soldiers were smiling.

382 put her net away. The only person who wasn't smiling was Father Vodol.

But then Father Christmas stopped smiling. And the reason he had stopped smiling was because he had just seen the clock on the wall. The clock said 'Most People's Bedtimes'.

'Right, elves, to the workshop! We've got a lot of toys to put in the infinity sack!'

And so Father Vodol was left alone, his face redder than the setting sun outside, as everyone – rabbits included – hurried off to the Toy Workshop to make Christmas happen.

An hour later Father Christmas was standing in the middle of the workshop, with his infinity sack open and a queue of elves and rabbits that stretched all the way back to Reindeer Field. As Rabbit 382 dropped a towering pile of toys into the sack, Father Christmas asked me to check on the sleigh, which was parked in front of his house, and to get the reindeer ready. So I did and all the reindeer made things easy for me, even Comet, who could be tricky with harnesses.

I looked at Blitzen. 'Now, whatever happens tonight, no diving through the air, okay?'

He made a truffling noise. Then I checked on the Barometer of Hope, which said 'Exceptionally Hopeful'.

I jumped into the sleigh and took the reins, and watched the queue of elves and rabbits get smaller and smaller until it eventually disappeared. And then Father Christmas arrived with his sack on his back. I handed him the reins and began to climb out of the sleigh.

'No, Amelia. You stay right there. I'll need a co-rider.'

'But you know what happened last time I was in a sleigh.'

'Yes, but Captain Soot isn't here now. Mary's looking after him. Look.'

And he waved at Mary, who was holding Captain Soot tightly. She was standing in the field with Noosh and Humdrum and Little Mim and Father Topo.

A crowd of elves were gathering around us now, ready for the take-off. Kip was among them. I started to panic. 'But what about someone else? What about Kip? He's the best sleigh rider in Elfhelm.'

Kip, overhearing, smiled at me and shook his head. 'I think it should be you. I know I was wrong about you. And I'm sorry.'

I sat back down.

'In fact,' said Father Christmas, 'you should be first.'

'What?'

He handed me the reins. 'Go on. Show them what you can do.'

'But . . .'

In the crowd I saw Twinkle, smiling and giving me the thumbs up. Snowflake was there too. And then I saw Father Vodol, hovering around like a dark cloud.

'You can do it, Amelia!' Mary shouted.

I looked at the Barometer of Hope and closed my eyes and believed very hard that everything was going to be all right.

'Come on, Blitzen!' I shouted. 'Come on, Vixen! Donner! Prancer! Dasher! Dancer! Cupid! Comet! Let's fly!'

And a moment later the crowd parted and

we were speeding across the snowy field towards the frozen lake and then up, up, up into the air, and we were on our way, around the world.

Just two happy humans who didn't really belong anywhere.

Father Christmas.

And me.

A Final Smile

I will always remember that Christmas Eve more than any other.

Father Christmas let me drive the sleigh the whole time, and all the reindeer – even Blitzen – behaved themselves. Though that was also the Christmas that a lot of human children and parents noticed footprints on carpets. At first – according to the letters Pippin caught all through the next year – they thought they were muddy footprints, but, leaning closer, they realised that they smelt rather nice. Rather chocolatey.

The next day, it was quite a strange sight seeing the rabbits and elves all feasting together as the Sleigh Belles sang 'Jingle Bells' and 'Hero In The Red Coat' and, of course, their classic 'Reindeer Over The Mountain'. It was a truly joyous time. And it remained joyous, all through the year.

The rabbits went down into their warren until Easter, because it was warmer down there, but elves often went down there too, and the first Saturday of every month became Colour

Worm Disco Day, where the Sleigh Belles would play alongside a rabbit band called the Burrow Brothers and another very loud group called Ears of Doom, with our old prison guard on drums, and everyone had a great time. Even after Easter, the rabbits stayed underground a lot of the time.

You might want to know about the chocolate too. Well, the chocolate was returned to the bank and everyone got their money back, but the Bank of Chocolate began to make three times as much chocolate as usual. Most of it was then given to the rabbits who worked in their artists' studios – formerly Father Vodol's secret newspaper factory – inside the warren designing beautiful eggs of all sizes.

Father Vodol wasn't locked up, because Father Christmas didn't believe in locking anyone up. He was kept under close watch in his house on Very Quiet Street, and was forced to close the *Daily Truth*, which no one wanted to read anyway, and instead he was put to work as Chief Christmas Wrapper. He had to sit in a special room in the workshop wrapping every single present. It was a particularly annoying job for Father Vodol as he kept on getting sticky tape stuck in his beard.

Mary kept working as route planner for Father Christmas and, later, took over the Figgy Pudding café and called it Mother Christmas's Magic Pie Place. It soon became the most popular café in town. She stayed very much in love with Father Christmas, and he with her. And their cheeks seemed to grow rosier with happiness every day.

Hope was back in the air. The Northern Lights shone bright. And the letters to Father Christmas always made it to the top of the mountain.

As for me, well, things got better. A lot better.

Elves didn't whisper about me any more. I was no longer the outsider. Elfhelm was a place that welcomed humans and rabbits alike. And school was better too. Mother Jingle and all the other teachers seemed to have more respect for me. Columbus even set me a special assignment – to write a new history of Elfhelm, correcting all the mistakes about rabbits. Twinkle and Snowflake became great friends, and didn't even laugh at me during spickle dancing classes any more.

By writing for the *Daily Snow* I managed, eventually, to pay for the repairs to the Blizzard 360. Kip and I even became friends, of sorts, and compared stories of our experiences of being kidnapped. I won the Junior Sleigh Rider of the Year competition, and wore my badge with pride.

After my article about Father Vodol and the Easter Bunny boosted sales of the newspaper to record levels, I was made Chief Rabbit Correspondent, and my interview with the Easter Bunny was declared the 'most heartbreaking read of the year' by everyone who read it.

And life went on like this for years. Well, more or less. Christmases came and went. Father Christmas stayed busy at the Toy Workshop and Mary stayed busy at the café and I stayed busy at school and at the *Daily Snow*, but it was a happy kind of busy. An elf kind of busy.

Years later, on a Christmas Day, I left Elfhelm after one last sleigh ride and returned to London to set up an orphanage, the Magical Home for Girls and Boys. The reason I decided to leave wasn't because I was unhappy. Quite the opposite. I have never been as happy anywhere as I was amid the magic of elves and Father Christmas.

I still remembered the time before – a time

when I was lonely and miserable, an orphan at the workhouse – and I knew there were other people just like me in the world of humans, feeling the same. And so I decided to be like Father Christmas. I decided to try to make people happy, give them clean beds, and good meals based on Mary's best recipes, and teach them how to read and write.

I often told the orphans the story of my childhood. After their afternoon cake I would sit by the fire on a winter's day and tell them about the time I'd spent in Elfhelm.

I would talk about elves and pixies and trolls. I would talk about Father Christmas and Mother Christmas and the Easter Bunny. I would tell them that their letters to Father Christmas flew all the way to Very Big Mountain and were caught by a brilliant acrobatic elf called Pippin, who was amazing at leaping and catching.

I still tell them these stories, even now, as an old woman Even in this world of new inventions like motorcars and flying machines called aeroplanes.

And, although I never go back to Elfhelm these days, I still feel the magic of those days. Even though I was never drimwicked, I still keep that magic alive by trying to make people happy. By seeing the goodness in people. And letting that goodness shine back.

As Father Christmas once said, 'Smiling is the best kind of magic in the world.'

And I am smiling now, this Christmas Day, as I sit here finishing this tale. His letter is right here beside me. The one he left for me, in the fireplace.

It said just a few words: 'Thank You, Amelia.'

That was all it said. And all it needed to say. Because words are a magic too, and they can contain everything.

The bit after the book where you thank people

It is quite hard, writing a book. Quite enjoyable too. But you need a lot of help, as a writer, before a book becomes a book. This is especially true of *Father Christmas and Me*, and the two books before it in the trilogy – *A Boy Called Christmas* and *The Girl Who Saved Christmas*.

In particular, I must thank:

You. The reader. I thought you read it very well. Not too fast, not too slow. Well done you.

Chris Mould. The illustrator. For putting amazing pictures everywhere. Books with nice pictures are the best books.

Francis Bickmore. My brilliant editor. For telling me which bits were worse than other bits, so I could make them better.

Clare Conville. My agent. For being wise and lovely.

Everyone at Canongate, who has worked so hard on these books. Including Rafi Romaya, Megan Reid, Rona Williamson, Jenny Fry, Claire Maxwell, Alice Shortland, Neal Price, Jane Pike, Andrea Joyce, Caroline Clarke, Christopher Gale and, not forgetting, Jamie Byng.

Andrea Semple. My best friend. Who read this book first, when all the mistakes were still in it. And who gets rid of the mistakes. And makes this and every book far better than it would be.

Oh, and thanks to Father Christmas. Obviously.

Mostly though, I need to thank the two most amazing children in the entire world. Pearl Haig and Lucas Haig. They are the reason I write these books. They add magic to my life on a daily basis. This is my attempt to add some of it back.

Thank you all.

Merry Christmas!